Goulart   288479

The sword swallower

THE SWORD SWALLOWER

THE SWORD SWALLOWER

BY RON GOULART

1968

DOUBLEDAY & COMPANY, INC., GARDEN CITY, N.Y.

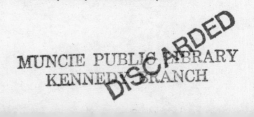

LIBRARY OF CONGRESS CATALOG CARD NUMBER 68–27120

FIRST EDITION

DEDICATION

TO my father, Joseph S. Goulart

THE SWORD SWALLOWER

ONE

THE old man danced on the wall. He grew larger, flickered, was gone.

The peach-colored office came light, the projection unit rattled to silence and the Head blinked his round wide eyes. "I'll tell you who that was," he said. He flicked a yellow disc out of a filigreed pillbox and positioned the disc on his tongue.

Ben Jolson, slouched on the visitor's side of the low black desk, said, "It's the man you want impersonated."

"That's right," said Head Mickens, swallowing and brightening. He rested a finger tip in the depression beneath his left eye. "The pressures that go with this job have really increased so much lately, Jolson. One of the big reasons is all that trouble with the War Bureau."

"You mean the disappearances?"

"Exactly," said Head Mickens, loosening the throat seam of his quiet blue tunic. "First it was General Moosman, followed by Admiral Rockisle. A week later Bascom Lamar Taffler, the father of Nerve Gas Number 414, vanishes from all ken. And now this morning, about the break of day, Dean Swift himself."

Jolson sat up. "The chairman of the War Bureau is missing?"

"It hasn't been leaked to any of the news media as yet. I'm breaking it to you, Jolson. Swift was last seen in the north corner of his rose garden. He's a great rose man."

"I saw a documentary about it," said Jolson. "So. You people in the Political Espionage Office have called on the Chameleon Corps because of the disappearances?"

"Yes," nodded Head Mickens. He unwrapped a blue and gold spansule and dropped the foil into the dispozhole next to his desk. "We've got us another explosive situation here. It goes without saying that our Barnum System of planets can't afford another peace scare."

"You suspect pacifists?"

The Head put his thumb in his ear and half rotated his palm. "We have little to go on, precious little in terms of hard factual input. I'll admit there is a tendency on the part of the Political Espionage Office to see pacifists everywhere. As you already know, there is a mounting objection to the way the War Bureau has been handling Barnum's annexing of the Terran planets."

"Particularly when they demolished North Dakota."

"One little state." The Head popped the spansule into his mouth. "At any rate, Jolson, you have to admit that when key War Bureau people, and War Bureau affiliates, start vanishing, well, it could indeed be pacifists."

Jolson asked, "Who exactly was the old man in the films?"

"Leonard F. Gabney," said the Head. He tapped the desk top with his spread finger tips. "I'm supposed to take something else, for the side effects."

Jolson reached down and picked a pill roll off the peach rug. "These?" he said, tossing.

"Let's hope so. Now, as to Gabney, Jolson. He himself is not important, just an old gentleman you'll be impersonating for us. He's big in the telekinesis industry here on Barnum and will be kept out of sight while you're using his identity. Anyway, you'll be sleepbriefed on him, backgrounded. Let's get to the actual assignment." Head Mickens tore a pill off the roll. "The important person in all this is Wilson A. S. Kimbrough."

Shaking his head, Jolson said, "Wait. Kimbrough is the ambassador to the planet Esperanza, isn't he?"

"Yes, he runs the Barnum Embassy in the capital there." The Head tilted slightly and blinked at Jolson.

"I don't want to go to Esperanza."

"Don't want to go?" asked the Head. "You have to go, Jolson. Once a Chameleon Corps man, always a Chameleon Corps man. Even though you're on the semi-active list now, you have to put duty before business. Plus which, we can fine you, get the lease on your ceramics plant canceled."

"Esperanza will unsettle me," said Jolson, slumping again in his chair.

"They have to bury people somewhere, Jolson."

"But a whole planet that's nothing but cemeteries," said Jolson.

"There are a couple million people on Esperanza," Head Mickens told him. "Alive people, living there. Not to mention, let me see, a million and a half tourists per year and well over half a million mourners." He held a memo up.

Jolson looked away. "The whole damn planet smells like floral pieces."

"Chances are you won't go near a cemetery or a wreath," said the Head of the Political Espionage Office. "Let me outline the specific assignment for you, Jolson. There is a possibility, and this is based on material gathered by our far-flung PEO agents, that Ambassador Kimbrough is linked up with this wave of War Bureau abductions. Admiral Rockisle was actually on Esperanza, to put a wreath on the grave of the Unknown Commando, when he vanished."

"Ambassador Kimbrough's tied in, huh?"

"This is one of many leads we have to check out," said Head Mickens. "If Kimbrough is a weak link we want to establish it. Starting next week he'll be spending a vacation period at Nepenthe, Inc., just outside Esperanza City."

"Nepenthe, Inc. That's the rejuvenation spa for old tycoons?"

"A sort of refuge and rehabilitation center for weary industrialists and political leaders, yes. Mostly old gentlemen in their eighties and nineties," said Mickens. "What we want to do is this. You change into this old boy Gabney, eighty-three himself, and we slip you into Nepenthe, Inc." He watched Jolson for a moment. "You won't have any trouble changing into old Gabney, will you?"

Jolson bowed his head over a palmed fist. "Nope," he said. He made a faint hunkering motion, his face blurring. Then he grinned evenly at Mickens. Jolson was old, in his eighties, crosshatched with thin wavery wrinkles. He rubbed at his sharp chin with one aged stiff hand. His black tunic crumpled in, puckering on his now thin chest.

The PEO man cleared his throat. "You'd think by now they'd have a way to make old age more presentable," he said. "Come back, you make me edgy. This medication regimen I'm on, Jolson, if followed correctly should keep me from ever looking like a Gabney."

Jolson's body shuddered for an instant and he was himself. "Maybe you can get the Chameleon Corps to process you, teach you to turn young."

"Nobody outside CC can get at the process. You know that, Jolson. Perhaps someday, though." Mickens sighed, went on more sharply. "Back to business."

"You want me just to listen at Nepenthe, Inc.?"

"No, we want you to get Ambassador Kimbrough alone as soon as you get a chance and hit him with a battery of truth drugs. Find out what he knows, all he knows, who he's tied in with and what their motives are."

Jolson rocked once. "Okay, I guess I have to do it."

"You'll be issued the standard portable truth kit. Hide it in your luggage till you get inside Nepenthe, then wear it under your arm. You know the drill on that."

"Who's my PEO contact on Esperanza?"

Head Mickens said, "I can't tell you at this time because of some new security procedures we're trying out. You'll be approached there."

"How?"

Head Mickens felt his desk top. "I have a special identifying phrase here someplace." He found a blue memo card. "Yes, this. 15–6–1–24–26–9–6. Got it? 15–6–1–24–26–9–6." He dealt the memo into the dispozhole. "On Esperanza someone will say, or more likely whisper, that number sequence to you."

"How come numbers. What happened to the poetry quotes?"

Mickens said, "Security thought they were too controversial. Besides, it's not very masculine to have agents running around saying, 'With how sad steps, O Moon, thou climb'st the skies,' and 'A violet by a mossy stone, half hidden from the eye!' and things of that nature."

"What's the length of my stay at Nepenthe likely to be?"

"We've booked you, as Leonard F. Gabney, in for a week," said Head Mickens. "Though we'd like results as soon as you can get them." He noticed a green memo punchcard. "The place costs ten thousand dollars a week, Jolson. We had to siphon some money out of the Political Espionage Office's recreation fund to pay your tab."

"There goes the hot lunch program."

"Not to mention the new handball court for computer programmers," said the Head. "But we can't cut costs. This is a crisis. What isn't around here? You're to report next to your Chameleon Corps Briefing Complex, Jolson. Oh, first help me find a vial of raspberry-colored liquid. I was supposed to take a spoonful a half hour ago."

They both got down on hands and knees.

TWO

THE yellow flagstone courtyard was warm with late morning sun. The palisades curved down to the deep green ocean in slaty jigsaws. Jolson relaxed in his tropical lounge-chair and let his chin rest on the rim of his maté cup. "You've got new music tracks in the mechanical birds," he said.

MacRae, a long big-boned Chameleon Corps captain, shook his head. "We put in real birds about a month ago, Ben." He upended a filing packet over the rec table and memory spools cascaded out. "Had some guy through from the Efficiency Squad. His report said real birds are more economical. So we got some."

Jolson elbowed lower in his chair and watched a flock of dark birds circle in the thin blue sky. "You're stationed right here on Barnum all the time now, Mac?"

"Yeah, I have a route," said MacRae, "doing two or three simple impersonations a week. Rest of the time I'm staff here at Briefing." He selected three Esperanza spools and sandwiched them, stacked them next to the data reels on Leonard F. Gabney. "You're leaving for Esperanza tonight, aren't you?"

"Ten, from the Keystone City port," said Jolson.

"Political Espionage has got all my big sleepbriefing machines tied up the rest of today and into tomorrow," said MacRae as he selected another trio of memory spools.

"I'll have to stick you in one of the roomettes. It's still got those old-style machines, like the ones we had back in the Chameleon Corps Academy. Remember?"

"Ten thousand words a minute playover," said Jolson, nodding. "With a retention average of about eighty-two per cent."

"Eighty-four per cent," said MacRae. He poured a fresh cup of maté for himself, scratched his ankle. "I think Political Espionage is planning another assassination, Ben. Probably out on Murdstone."

"That's three on Murdstone this year."

"The problem Political Espionage is having is that the pacifist forces keep assassinating the men PEO shoves in to replace the guys they've assassinated," MacRae said. "All this pacifist stuff, assassinations, counter revolutions. Things aren't simple like when we first got into the Chameleon Corps, Ben. Sometimes I think maybe I'm going to try to go on semi-active duty, take half pay. Ten years with the CC, it's not like ten years anywhere else." He knuckled his knee. "You're semi-retired, aren't you, Ben?"

"Yeah," said Jolson. "I'm trying to run a wholesale pottery business. I don't know, though; since we're permanently on call for a certain number of these damn Chameleon Corps assignments it's probably better to stay on full-time duty. At least the pay is better full-time."

"I have a theory that maybe half-time crap is better than full-time crap," said MacRae. "I was looking at your records. You're a Lieutenant Two now. I never thought they'd let you make a rank even that high, Ben. PEO always used to needle CC about you." He smiled. "The way you used to refuse to stop playing the roles. Where was it that time, on Peregrine wasn't it? Yeah, where you wouldn't stop being the ruler of the jungle kingdom. Stayed there an extra six months because you said you liked the outdoor work."

"I was restless in my twenties."

"You were a piano or something once, too, in a bordello satellite orbiting Murdstone," said MacRae. "They had to get a team of movers to haul you off that assignment."

Standing, Jolson finished off his maté. "I'm settling into things more now, Mac. Middle age comes on early in this Barnum climate. I'm almost thirty-one, mellowing."

"Easy time," said MacRae. "You've got to learn to do easy time. You went into the Academy young. It must have been, what, twenty years ago?"

"Nearly," said Jolson. "I was twelve."

"Your father got you a special appointment to the Chameleon Corps Academy, didn't he? He was a mayor someplace."

"Governor," said Jolson.

MacRae stacked the Esperanza and Gabney spools together. "What planet?"

"This one, another territory."

The Chameleon Corps Briefing Complex was low and rambling, an intricacy of raw metal, raw wood and panels, circles and squares of opaque-colored nearglass. Behind it sloping hills stretched, empty of other buildings, brightly green. MacRae walked toward the nearest door. "Ever see him?"

"No," said Jolson. He stepped inside after MacRae.

The body of the old briefing machine was dappled, silver and black. Jolson thought, easing into sleep, of old

Dr. Anthony H. Davis-Stockbridge. Hands in coat vents, wide rounded back pressed against a dappled machine, Davis-Stockbridge would reminisce. He'd been in his high nineties then, senility starting to work on him.

"Initially my concern was for the therapy factors and play values," Dr. Davis-Stockbridge said. A shape changer himself, he had difficulty now in remembering his identity completely. There would be days when his face was lean, his hair silver; others when he'd be shorter, with a half-moon chin and a pink bare head. Today he seemed almost right, except for a wispy yellow beard.

The scattering of Chameleon Corps Academy cadets in the model sleepbriefing room listened carefully, quietly. Davis-Stockbridge had invented the process that made the CC possible.

"The Cole Foundation," the old doctor told them, "had indicated, sworn in fact, that their interest in the Davis-Stockbridge process was entirely for its psychiatric values. I had wanted to use it primarily in dealing with identity fragmentations. The role playing was of obvious value. Even at the age of forty, which I then was, I was not aware, as I should have been, that the Political Espionage Office was paying me. Paying me through the Cole Foundation. PEO had nothing but espionage motives, had the formation of the Chameleon Corps in mind always. From the start. To you young men, you who are mastering the passade, the art of passing quickly and completely from role to role, it must seem difficult to accept the long processing necessary to make the swift transition possible."

Davis-Stockbridge's beard was gone, his face a bit thinner. "Unless one wishes dangerous mutagenic effects, however, the conditioning must be gradual. I realize now the very length of the transfiguration training would likely rule out the use of the Davis-Stockbridge process for any psychiatric, or probably even entertainment, purpose. To control the alpha beams was one of the very real difficulties, as you young men no doubt realize. We had many unfortunate transmogrifications, long ago. Many years in the past. Once I had determined that a series of operations on the pineal gland would facilitate identity transformations I was able, however, to progress at a much faster rate, gentlemen. The passade was also improved. Still there is little likelihood the Davis-Stockbridge process would have reached any truly functional, in Political Espionage Office terms, any truly functional stage had I not, almost by accident, found that a simple mixture of chlorpheniramine maleate, phenylpropanolamine hydrochloride and isopropamide in capsule form, ingested daily over a prolonged period, had the exact metaphrastic factors needed."

Slowly Dr. Davis-Stockbridge's beard was returning. He said, "Certainly the intense psychological conditioning that stabilizes the basic identity while allowing it to alter its outward form is of value as well, a notion all you young men will no doubt say Aye to. Certainly, too, there is no denying that the several secret ingredients to which I hold the key play their part. We have arrived in an area where the Political Espionage Office would appreciate more confiding on my part. Although I at times have the notion they have already, with their knack for using truth drugs so well, have already found out all my secrets. Every one. I hope, gentlemen, I hope my secrets are still mine. One would like to think so."

Jolson said something to himself, came awake to listen. He squinted, ran a hand over his dry mouth. He sat up, grimacing, on the tufted briefing room cot. "Huh," he said.

MacRae, his watch to his ear, said, "Should do it, Ben. Not as thorough as it could be, but you should know enough about Esperanza and Gabney to get along fine."

Jolson swung off the cot, stretched. "One would like to think so," he said.

THREE

THE wheelchair was lost down a humid side ramp under the spaceport. "Heck," its grid voice said. "I was sure Visitor Processing was just around that last turn. Okay now, stick with me. We'll find her."

"Thunderation," said Jolson. "I don't need a contraption like you anyway. Release me and I'll trot up to the proper area."

The chair tightened the safety belt around Jolson's low round stomach. "Esperanza Spaceport Number Two has a policy of providing courtesy rides for all you elder citizens. Stick with me, I'm getting a hunch."

Jolson was Leonard F. Gabney, bent and brittle, freckled with age. His voice had a thin, about-to-cough sound. "Damnation," he told the robot chair, "what kind of planet is this when they can't even build an adequate andy chair."

"Easy, easy. I know where we are now," the chair told him. "I recognize that mural. We're on the trail again."

The mural was done in faintly glowing colors on black nearcloth, a montage of the better-known tombs. Shivering, Jolson said, "Morbid. Whole planet is morbid."

"Sometimes I feel that way too," said the chair. "You think this is bad, you ought to work out in the cemeteries themselves. I was ten years showing tourists around. It's kind of silly for a machine to be superstitious but I used to get the willies out there. To me it's bad luck to walk over a grave, or roll over one in my case."

"I'm here on your blasted planet for my health," said Jolson. "I don't intend to visit one single solitary damned cemetery."

"We never know when we're going to," said the chair. "Well, don't let me upset you with my chatter. Ten years out in the cemeteries, you get to thinking. Here comes Corridor Fourteen. See, I told you I'd get you there."

"My ship touched down a good hour ago," Jolson complained. "A good hour ago."

The wheelchair braked in front of a low metallic counter and unbuckled. "Out in the cemeteries I could guide myself by the sun and familiar landmarks, certain fixed stars after nightfall. All these corridors down here, you lose track. Nice to have served you, Mr. Grobney."

"Gabney, Leonard F. Gabney, you impudent machine." Jolson stood, adjusted his loose musty suit and walked over to the counter tabbed Visitor Processing: DAV-HOB. He tapped hard on the counter top with one dry gnarled hand.

"Now to find my way back to Gate AA," said the departing chair.

"Well?" said Jolson and repeated the counter tapping.

A ceiling-hung monitoring eye aimed itself at him. A speaker dangling next to it said, "Calm down, grandaddy. What's your name?"

"Everyone knows me. I'm Leonard F. Gabney and I feel I've spent quite a sufficient amount of time in this overheated labyrinth."

"Calm down, grandaddy. All G arrivals are being temporarily handled up on Level Two. Take the corridor here to its end. The ramp will carry you on up."

Jolson snorted. "Not only morbid, but not efficient."

"Calm down, grandaddy."

On the rising ramp a thin young man with tight curling blond hair put his arm through Jolson's. "You a G, too?"

"I'm Leonard F. Gabney, you young whelp, and stop fondling me."

"Oh, look, I'm not trying anything odd," said the young man. "No, sir. You're the telekinesis king, aren't you, Mr. Gabney? I'm Peter Terraloma Gooden, home planet Earth. In the Earth System. You've maybe heard of my planet, sir?"

"I own a great part of it," said Jolson. "Unwind yourself from me."

"You looked all in," said Gooden. "I'm actually only trying to be of service. Too many young people today go around looking shabby, being loudmouthed and ignoring our young old-timers. I think we ought to respect our senior citizens, our golden yearers."

"At least the old coots with a bankroll like mine," said Jolson.

"Seriously, sir," said Gooden. "I happen to know Barnum is your planet of origin, but I do feel that on Earth in the Earth System we have a sincere, genuine respect for our old-timers. You'll notice I call it the Earth System and not the so-called Solar System. If Earth had its rightful place, Mr. Gabney, things wouldn't be so botched up out here in the other systems."

"Oh, so?"

"I don't go so far as to back some of these Earth supremacy people, or pacifist guys who never shave," said Gooden. "Yet you have to admit they come up with some good ideas."

"About these newer ideologies I know nothing," Jolson said casually.

"I've said enough under that heading, I guess, sir. How's the telekinesis business going these days?"

"Can't complain," said Jolson. "Do you work for a living?"

"I haven't told you, excuse me. Yes; I'm with the Derelict Research Foundation."

"A charitable organization, is it?"

The ramp reached a peak and started downhill. "Not exactly, Mr. Gabney. What we in the Derelict Research Foundation, a company started right on old Earth, do is motivational studies among the down and out. There's a sizable down-and-out population on Esperanza, though you're not going to learn much about it in the tourist promos."

"I certainly hope I can avoid any direct contact with derelicts."

"Sure, stay out of the Fringe and you don't have to worry much," said Gooden. "The point is, many manufacturers overlook the derelict entirely. DRF has research to indicate the buying power of all the derelicts in the Barnum System exceeds a half a billion a year. It's mostly throwaway money, too."

"Indeed," said Jolson. "What sort of products are you trying to interest these undesirables in?"

"Right at the moment it's mostly drugs and wine," said Gooden. "After this present trip I'm going to be able to work out marketing plans for some other cartels. You may not know it, Mr. Gabney, but it was some of my research that led to the introduction of the bouncing wine bottle out here."

"Which is?"

Gooden chuckled and said, "I found one of the big derelict complaints was falling over with a wine bottle in their pockets and suit vents. Cheap wine manufacturers for the Barnum System were still using a nearglass container. I told them to put their wine in unbreakable bottles. Sales have upped twenty-two per cent. Thanks to me a derelict can fall down in a gutter with a feeling of confidence. People like a product they can trust. Same thing can be said in the telekinesis field, can't it, sir?"

The ramp deposited them in front of an android-staffed customs counter and in a few minutes Jolson's passport was flicked through and punched and his luggage was set on a small hoverdolly. A wall panel near the counter then slid open and a girl in a vinyl tartan uniform stepped toward Jolson.

"Welcome, Mr. Gabney. I'm from the Esperanza Spaceport Number Two Travel Haven Lodge, sent here to guide you to your rooms. The landcruiser from Nepenthe, Inc., will be arriving after the dinner hour to transport you there. Meantime, we'll make you snug and comfortable as can be."

"I won't ride in any more wheelchairs."

"That's right," the snub-nosed girl said, leading him into another warm corridor.

"Too stuffy," said Jolson. "I hope this whole blasted planet isn't stuffy."

"Sometimes the outside air pollution, which exists in Esperanza City only in perfectly safe amounts, gets into the port air-conditioning mechanisms. It's osmosis."

"Thunderation," said Jolson.

"That's right," said the girl.

FOUR

JOLSON was watching his right foot, inscribing lazy arcs with it on the processed air of his spaceport suite. Above the view dome in the ceiling of his Senior Citizen Wing cabana the sky was a thick yellow. "You folks certainly haven't solved your atmosphere problems," he said to the room. "We wouldn't tolerate messy air like that on Barnum."

"Sure thing, gramps," said a wall speaker.

Jolson's hands sank deeper into his trouser slits. After running his tongue around in his cheek, he said, "Thunderation. What's keeping that drink I ordered?"

"No hard stuff for you," the grid told him. "It's on your medicard, gramps. Why don't you try the hot soup outlet in your sleep area?"

"Balderdash," said Jolson. He'd been here an hour now and no one from the Political Espionage Office had contacted him.

"Venusian gumbo's the special today."

"Bah."

"Watch some entertainment then while you're waiting for the Nepenthe, Inc., wagon to come for you."

The dimensional pedestal across from Jolson hummed and a sinewy white-haired man materialized. "Old Man Cushman with another segment of the Geriatrics Network's special Senior Citizen Show," he announced. He was wearing a loose orange uniform and from a pocket he hoisted out a model of a many-storied building. "Here's a souvenir of Esperanza that lots of thoughtful old-timers are sending back home to their grandchildren. You may not believe this, ladies and gentlemen, but this is a perfect scale model of one of Esperanza City's justly famed funspires. It's filled with flavorful kid doses of migraine reliever and you can teleport it anywhere in the Barnum System for practically pennies."

"I told you I didn't want to view that godawful thing," cried Jolson. "Thunderation."

"Watch the language, gramps," said the grid.

The pedestal hummed and Old Man Cushman was snuffed out.

"Go to blazes," muttered Jolson. "Damned patronizing room."

"Hey," shouted the grid. "You shouldn't ought to talk in such a way to me. How'd you like to step out in the hallway, gramps?"

"If I did you'd still be mounted in the wall," said Jolson.

"You're a great one for picking on a person's handicaps. What do you care about a speaker grid. Means nothing to you."

"Look, are you going to order me a drink or not?" Jolson drummed the fingers of one spotted hand on the arm of his chair. "I recall a suite at the Murdstone Ritz where a man could bribe the servomechanisms."

The grid made a pouting noise, finally said, "Why should I do a mean old ginzo like you a favor? Still, if you drop ten bucks in realmoney down the shoeshine outlet you can probably get a drink in a jiffy, gramps."

Jolson tottered to his feet, found the money in his cash pouch. He was poised directly over the hole in the floor when the suite door chimed. "Yes?" he said.

"Welcome to Esperanza on behalf of the Barnum Embassy in Esperanza City," called a girl's voice. "I have a welcoming basket of reconstituted fruit for you, Mr. Leonard F. Gabney. As part of the Barnum Embassy's special service to all important new arrivals from Barnum."

"Well, well, my dear," said Jolson as he got the door open.

Standing there, lips very slightly parted, was a young willowy brunette. She had sharply angled cheekbones, shoulder-length hair and was standing a bit on tiptoe. Her dress was lemon yellow, with a Barnum Embassy crest over her right breast. Across the girl's forehead the numbers 15-6-1-24-26-9-6 were written small in lipstick. "We greet all prominent Barnum visitors such as yourself," she said, winking one smoky hazel eye and quickly wiping her tanned forehead clean with a plyochief. "I'm Jennifer Hark, Mr. Gabney," she said and came sideways into the suite.

"Indeed you are, young lady," said Jolson. The door closed itself and Jolson added, "So?"

She jerked her head negatively and walked out onto the small round enclosed patio. Putting the fruit basket down on a lounging mat, the girl passed her hand under the mat and then motioned Jolson out. "I've got a bug-killing device in the basket. Which'll knock out any mike pickups and sound guns," she explained when he joined her.

"Who'd be listening to me? Besides the Senior Citizen andies."

"They can be dangerous enough," the girl said. "Not

only them. Any number of other groups may be monitoring these rooms. It's best to follow security procedures whenever possible. The fruit in the basket is dummy stuff, masking equipment specially designed to fritz any nearby bugs."

"Won't the hotel get suspicious?"

"I'm only here for a few moments." From the basket Jennifer chose a runt apricot and handed it to Jolson. "Keep this with you. If you get in trouble at Nepenthe, Inc., squeeze it."

"And have a glass of apricot juice?"

"There's a signaling device inside the thing. You give it a squeeze and I'll come and help you out of whatever fix you're in. See?"

"Wait," said Jolson. "I don't need any lady daredevils to help me." He thumbed the fruit at her.

Jennifer pushed it back. "Political Espionage Office orders. You're to keep it with you at all times."

"I'm going to look great at a spa carrying an apricot around."

"Tell them it's a fetish. Old men have lots of those." The girl cocked her head and studied Jolson. "This is really wonderful. You look ninety."

"Eighty-three and don't call me gramps."

One of her long-fingered hands spun out and touched at his face. "You're really old. How do you do it?"

"It's a knack you pick up."

She smiled, a quiet smile. "Ben Jolson. One time on Peregrine you posed as the leader of a band of desert raiders, did it for two months longer than your assignment called for. I think that's a romantic side many Chameleon Corps men don't share."

"Desert air is good for your sinuses," said Jolson. "Is all this stuff about me given out in some kind of publicity kit by CC? Or do you have your own dossier on me?"

"A man I used to know in PEO let me read the back files," Jennifer said. "He had a portable code reader and we'd do it on long dismal weekends. Ben Jolson."

"Yeah," he said. "Now what do you have to tell me?"

She rested the fingers of one hand on her cheek. "We've got nothing much more on Ambassador Kimbrough, except a fairly certain rumor he's got a sizable unexplained bank account in a satellite bank orbiting Tarragon. Two hundred thousand dollars on the ledger tapes."

"Nothing to link him more definitely to the War Bureau disappearances?"

"Only what you were briefed," said the slim girl. "We are starting to pick up veiled references to something called Group A." She sat on the edge of a rocking chair, stretching her long legs straight in front of her.

Letting the apricot tumble into a trouser slit, Jolson asked, "Group A, huh? And they're involved with these snatches?"

"Let's say it's a possibility that has to be checked out."

"PEO has an idea some pacifist group is maybe in on the War Bureau abductions," said Jolson. "Could Group A be a pacifist gang?"

"We don't know," said Jennifer. "We're not absolutely certain they're tied in at all. When you go up against Ambassador Kimbrough see what he has to say about Group A."

"Okay," said Jolson.

"You got your truth kit through all right?" the girl asked.

When he nodded she said, "I hope you'll get a clear chance to use it."

"I may not have to," said Jolson. "You can find things out easier ways. Do you really work at the Embassy?"

"It's my cover," the brunette said. "I'm one of the ones who supplied the early hints, some, that Ambassador Kimbrough might be up to no good. Something unethical and possibly even treason. That's a tough thing to be sure of. To weed out the usual civic and political graft and kickback from the more dangerous kinds." She smiled and her cheeks hollowed for an instant. "Kimbrough's been involved in the usual kind of mildly illegal things, too. A muckraking reporter named Sol S. Mahones uncovered one of those and even that grandstand wall TV newsman, Floyd Janeway, picked it up. You remember, the satellite Kimbrough had launched just to celebrate his second wife's twentieth birthday."

"Sure, which may not mean he's got anything to do with the War Bureau trouble at all."

Jennifer's head dipped and raised. She stood up, stretched without raising her arms. "We'll find out for sure pretty soon I think. Contact me if you need me to pull you out of any trouble out at Nepenthe, Inc. Should your mission run smoothly you're to get in touch with me on your return to Esperanza City. Go to the New Rudolph Flower Shop on Solitude Way, order one dozen yellow roses and repeat the identifying numbers. Any more questions?"

Jolson returned her fruit basket. "I can't quite place that scent you're wearing. What is it?"

"Called Golliwog, a teleport." She smiled again at him. "Be sure and signal when there's trouble."

Jolson took her arm with his wrinkled old hand. "I'm sorry, my dear, that a serious allergic condition prevents my accepting your kind basket. Even though I would wish it otherwise, the time for my afternoon nap has all but arrived."

The door to the corridor opened at Jolson's touch and Jennifer Hark left, walking crisply away.

"Damnation," he told the room, "why hasn't anything been done about my drink?"

"They insist on money in front," said the wall speaker. "That wasn't such a bad-looking girl. What I could see of her while she was in here."

"Yes, a splendid-looking young person, by dab," said Jolson.

"I usually don't like them skinny."

Jolson dropped some money into the floor hole.

FIVE

JOLSON stepped out of the pale blue landcruiser and into a pool of hot mud. He sank slowly down to chin level, frogged up and noticed a square-faced straight-haired man squatting and smiling on the broad pool's edge.

The man extended a hand. "We start things right off here at Nepenthe, Inc.," he said. "Shake, and welcome aboard. This mud dip has taken weeks of aging off you already, Mr. Gabney. I'm Franklin T. Tripp himself, Co-Ordinator and Partial Founder."

Jolson gave Tripp a muddy right hand. His cruiser driver had undressed him first, so he'd been expecting something. "I admire the quickness with which you start your therapy, sir."

"I'll tell you something, Mr. Gabney," Tripp confided in a scented voice. "I'm way over fifty years of age myself. Do I remotely look it?"

"Forty at best."

"Every chance I get I come out here and wallow." Tripp helped Jolson extract himself from the mud and then guided him down the blue-tiled path that curved around the pool.

It was a quiet dark night and Nepenthe was on the top of a plateau many miles beyond Esperanza City. The wind that moved across it was warm and dry. "I'm sure you'll be a real source of rejuvenation to me," said Jolson. "Not to mention inspiration."

"Ahead of you now, Mr. Gabney, is a little get-to-know-people session, where you meet folks. We've got a pretty nice guest list this stretch."

Behind them an attendant in a blue jumpsuit was dumping Jolson's luggage from the landcruiser. Jolson glanced at the piece of luggage that concealed the truth kit, back at Tripp. "I don't mingle at my best when I'm naked and muddy."

"We have no conventions here," said Tripp. "However, you will have a shower and get into one of our universal night robes first. Then report to the health lounge on Level One for a welcome in." He rubbed some mud off the speaker of his watch and put it to his ear. "Yes, a brief socializing session and then you'll turn in. We rise at an early, healthful hour here at Nepenthe, Inc., Mr. Gabney. Actually I owe the fact that I still have the mind and body of a boy to getting up with the sun."

"That and mud."

"Exactly." Tripp prodded Jolson through a bronzed door marked Welcoming Showers. "I'll leave you to your cleansing."

The shower room was long and blue, the floor a soft warm cushiony material. It was empty, flanked by two dozen shower outlets. Sitting on a straight nearwood chair in the far doorway was a wide bristly man in blue overalls, blue jersey. There was an old-fashioned papercover book steepled on his knee. "Where's your special health sandals, old man?"

"I don't have any," said Jolson. "I just arrived, young fellow."

The man got up, flexing various parts of himself at once, gently placing the open book on the chair seat. "Nat

Hockering is my name. Where's your health sandals, I asked you?"

Jolson clenched his weathered hands. "I'm newly arrived, escorted here by your own Mr. Tripp."

"Nobody takes a shower without special sandals. It's a health hazard otherwise."

"I would like to get this mud off."

"Sure you would, old man, but you're not going to. Gather your stringy old butt together and back out the way you came."

"Perhaps," said Jolson, "I could purchase the proper shoes."

"Where you got the money hidden?"

"I need hardly point out that a man without considerable means would not come here to Nepenthe."

"Twenty bucks for the shoes," said Hockering. "Give me the twenty at the start of the obstacle course tomorrow at nine sharp. A deal, old man?"

"You have the word of Leonard F. Gabney."

"For what that's worth," said Hockering. He reached around his doorway, snatched a pair of compo sandals and skimmed them over the floor to Jolson. "Nine on the nose, don't forget."

Bending, Jolson tugged the shoes on. "I had expected more cordiality here."

"You'll get it, only not from me. I'm just biding my time until I can get to a good multiversity and study architecture." He waved the book at Jolson. "Do you know anything about balustrades?"

"As much as the next man." Jolson moved under a water outlet. The mud was starting to cake. After scratching his round stomach he reached up and thumbed the ON toggle.

Nothing happened. "How does one go about getting water?"

"Hot or cold?" asked Hockering, who was back sitting. "Warm."

"Five dollars for any water after official shower closing time."

"And when did the showers close?"

"Shortly before you creaked in," said Hockering. "Hot water is ten dollars. Want to spring for that?"

"Yes, put it on my tab."

"I'm gambling I can trust you," said Hockering as the hot water began.

Three old men were in the Level One health lounge, a domed blue room with tube chairs and a nearjuice serving unit. Tripp was not present.

"My name is Leonard F. Gabney," Jolson announced, settling into a chair and adjusting his blue knee-length night robe. "Newly arrived from my home planet of Barnum."

The youngest old man, pink and round, grinned and made a toasting motion with his juice cup. I'm Phelps H. K. Sulu from Barafunda. I'm phasing myself out of the moss development line. Your field?"

"Telekinesis," said Jolson.

"You're that Gabney then," said Sulu. "I recall I once viewed a profile documentary about you, done by that crusading Janeway fellow."

"How," asked a straight tan old man, "do you stand?"

"Not as well as I used to," said Jolson. "Why?"

"I mean in a political, positional sense. How do you stand, sir?"

"On what?"

"You may begin anywhere," said the stiff man. "We'll eventually want complete backgrounding on you."

"This is Wing Commander Eberhardt," said Sulu. "He still has a preoccupation with political shadings. He's been at Nepenthe, without a break and at his family's expense, for nearly five years."

"Confusion to the pacifists," said the Wing Commander. "Take the Terra situation, Gabney, what are your feelings about that, sir?"

"I might agree with your position," said Jolson. "Since I have had a long and sincere admiration for the military mind."

"Excellent so far," said Wing Commander Eberhardt. "Let me ask you next how you stand in regard to the fact that there is a small green bug crawling along the tip of your nose."

Jolson made a flicking motion. "Oh, so?"

Wing Commander Eberhardt, rising, said, "I believe in turning in at approximately this time each evening. If there is no opposition?" He waited a few seconds, nodded and moved straightly out of the room.

The third old man spoke now. "Let me welcome you," he said, a lanky dusky man with close-cropped gray hair. "I haven't had a chance to speak up. As a native of Barnum myself I'm happy to greet you. I'm Wilson A. S. Kimbrough, serving, as you may know, as ambassador to Esperanza. I hope we can kick a few conversations around and perhaps I can be of help to you."

Jolson smiled.

SIX

HIS waking hand touched a waffle. It was card-size, plyobagged, resting on his sunken chest. The narrow contour bed was shaking Jolson awake, with accelerating agitation, and the wall and ceiling light strips were coming alive. The shutter panels on the view window runneled open to show a quiet comfortless dawn.

With the heel of his old man's hand Jolson tried to push himself upright and awake. The bed's restraining gear kept him fast. Gong notes came out of the room announcement grids. "Up and doing," came Franklin T. Tripp's voice. "First, however, let's make sure we all eat, chewing thoroughly and carefully, our usual morning one-minute dental hygiene waffle."

Jolson sighted along his wrinkled chin at the wrapped waffle. "Ugh," he said.

"The waffle shape," said Tripp in the speaker. "If we all realized the waffle shape is the perfect shape we'd live forever and a day."

Jolson clutched the packaged dental waffle, unseamed the bag and popped the thing in his mouth. When he had chewed the mint-flavored waffle thoroughly and carefully for a full minute the bed unleashed him and nudged him onto the padded floor.

After getting into his all-purpose blue exersuit, Jolson went cautiously into the corridor. Everything out here was soft blue. From the room next to his Wing Commander Eberhardt was emerging backwards. The Wing Commander hopped into the corridor, about-faced. "A strategic move I learned in the grim jungles of plucky little Murdstone, sir. Where do you stand on the North Dakota incident?"

"We discussed most of that last evening."

"Opinions change, change constantly," said Wing Commander Eberhardt. "I myself, when I could remember how to get those dictadesks to work, issued daily position papers."

"I had in mind talking to Ambassador Kimbrough about that very topic," said Jolson. "He's in 56B, isn't he, Wing Commander?"

"Yes, east of here, two corridors over," Eberhardt said. "However, you've no time for seeing him now. The drill is an organic steam treatment at once, Gabney. Come, let's trot along or Tripp will send attendants to fetch us. What branch of the military were you in, Gabney?"

"Commandos," said Jolson.

Wing Commander Eberhardt locked arms with him. "My late father, Subaltern Eberhardt, was a commando. No man was better at personal camouflage than Subaltern Eberhardt. Trees were his specialty. Had he not developed hay fever he would have risen much higher."

From under a bronzed door steam was seeping. Above the door beads of colored light spelled out Steam Club. "We undergo this every morning?" asked Jolson.

Wing Commander Eberhardt burst into the club, towing Jolson. "Don't underestimate the value of steam, and the waffle shape." He swung in close to Jolson's ear. "How do you stand, by the way, on the whole idea of steam, sir?"

Tripp himself took Jolson away from the Wing Commander. He guided Jolson into the steam-thick room and positioned him at a table. "Five minutes of intense organic steam," said Tripp, "and the age particles disperse, Mr. Gabney. To prove that organic steam therapy does work I've designed this special Steam Club, which combines the facilities and health potential of a standard steam room with the more exciting aspects of a private key club."

A tall, glistening green Venusian girl parted the swirls of steam. She was wearing only decalcomanias and had high-piled gold-flecked hair. "This dance is girl's choice, Mr. Gabney," she said. "Will you join me?"

"Shouldn't I have a little more steam first?"

"We can sit one out then," said the girl. Tripp retracted into the steam and the girl took his place. "I'll summon a waiter?"

"Certainly, my dear," said Jolson. "What would you like?"

"A waffle," the girl said. "It's all you can get here."

Jolson stroked the back of his wrinkled neck, watched the thick steam. "I was hoping to catch Ambassador Kimbrough here and jaw some about our mutual planet."

"He was through and out minutes ago."

Out of the whiteness Phelps H. K. Sulu and a polka-dotted Martian girl came bouncing. Sulu grinned and danced away.

"I would like to catch the ambassador before too long," said Jolson. "Sentiment over one's home planet, it grows strong as one ages."

"A few days on steam and waffles and you'll feel better," said the girl. "That damn waiter, it's too late now. You'll have to move on, Mr. Gabney, since five minutes of organic steam is all a fellow of your age can take. Ask for me again tomorrow. I like you. My name is Marissa." She noticed the butterfly over her left nipple was loose and reaffixed it.

His hand on a bronzed lever in a blue wall, Tripp said, "Ready for your jelly dip?"

"More waffles?" asked Jolson, who'd just had a centrifugal tumble to cap his hydroelectric six-android massage.

"It's you we dip." Tripp raised his eyebrows and his forehead rippled. "Sinking the body in a jelly substance takes a minimum of a hundred million aging particles from the surface of the skin, drives them right away."

"What sort of jelly is it?"

"Today it's apricot pineapple," said Tripp. "We change the flavor twice a week. All the jelly is made up a cup to a cup, a cup of sweetener to a cup of fruit. That's the important thing in this kind of war-on-aging therapy of mine. A cup to a cup." He twisted his wrist on the lever.

Jolson dropped down a chute and into a regulation-size pool filled with jelly. It was apricot pineapple.

Chinning himself out of the pool at its far end was Ambassador Kimbrough. Jolson called out but the ambassador didn't turn.

By the time Jolson worked his way to that end Kimbrough was long gone. A cold needle shower washed the jelly away in a drafty corridor beyond the pool. Dressed again and alone, Jolson ran, hoping to catch up with the ambassador.

An ankle-high trip rope caught him at the next doorway and Jolson went down, sprawling into a small dingy room.

Handing him a stout nearwood cane, a plump pale android said, "Curmudgeon therapy time, pappy."

"What?"

Three more fat andies stood behind this one. "A two-minute exercise period, pappy. You whack us with canes, thereby getting all those built-up emotional poisons out of your withered old carcass."

"I'll pass it this time."

A plump android stepped up and booted Jolson in the knee. "You are going to be nothing," he said, "but a big old sack of emotional poisons unless you use Mr. Tripp's own perfected system for quickly and easily ridding the body of trouble."

Jolson's fingers curved on the cane. He back-footed and swung the heavy stick. "Thunderation," he said. "Get out of my way, the lot of you."

"That's the way, pappy."

Jolson pivoted and whacked one android down. He clubbed the remaining ones and continued on after the ambassador.

Kimbrough was sitting in the Spiritual Cocktail Vestry, inserting a chargecard in one of the pedestaled mystic figures. Jolson started across the musky room for him.

The squatting android raised one of its pointing arms. "Harken," it spoke. "The secret of the universe, of this universe, of any universe really, is . . ."

Nat Hockering popped out of an alcove and made a stopping motion. "It's nearly nine. Come on and pay up, like you promised last night. Your dried-up old brain does remember you owe me thirty-five dollars, doesn't it?"

"Thirty," said Jolson, starting to bypass the big attendant.

Hockering blocked him. "See? Senility has really got you by the balls. You can't even remember, old man, how much you owe me and it was only last night you ran up the tab. Thirty-five dollars, Mr. Gabney."

Jolson fingered a money clip out of a trouser slit. "Here." Kimbrough was still attentive before the preaching android. "Leave me to contemplate," Jolson said. "I understand it's very good for wiping away time's ravages."

"May well be," said Hockering. "Right now it's breakfast time and the vestry is going to close up tight." With an armlock he took Jolson to breakfast.

SEVEN

AS they both sailed over the low hurdle Franklin T. Tripp said, "Running and jumping, Mr. Gabney, if only we all did more of it. I really think the fact I'm often mistaken for a youth in his late twenties is due to the large amount of running and jumping I do."

Jolson hit the turf, panting an old man's wheeze. "More important than mud and waffles?"

"As important," said Tripp. "As important."

"I imagine the perspiring has something to do with it."

A dozen of the old men were working around a half-mile track that was studded with hurdles and water obstacles.

"Sweating," said Tripp, who didn't seem to be winded. "Four entire years were wiped from my age by sweating alone."

An old man who had introduced himself as Olden Griggs at breakfast screamed somewhere behind them.

Tripp slowed to a trot. "Sounds like another of Griggs's seizures," he said. "You solo jog from this point and I'll drop back and clear the old fellow from the course."

Alone, Jolson stepped up his pace, trying to catch up with Ambassador Kimbrough, who he'd sighted several hundred yards ahead of him. He jumped a three-foot vinyl barrier, sprinted, leaped a box hedge. Found himself alongside Wing Commander Eberhardt.

"How," asked the Wing Commander, "do you stand on thermometers?"

"Neutral."

Wing Commander Eberhardt's elbows swung up chin high as he trotted. "They stuck one in me just prior to the start of this jaunt. Opinion is I can't be trusted with them orally, that I'll champ off the ends."

"Oh," said Jolson. He dashed ahead, leaped a pond. But he didn't get a chance to even speak to Kimbrough until they were put side by side in organic steam cabinets almost an hour later.

"Is the whole day programmed for us?" he asked the ambassador.

"There is," answered Kimbrough, "a free recreational period following the early afternoon enforced nap." He exhaled upward, puffing. "You wouldn't by any chance happen to be an archery buff, Gabney?"

Jolson said, "Archery is my first love, Kimbrough."

"That's marvelous," smiled the ambassador. "I've had the devil's own time finding anyone to get out on the range with me. Yesterday, in fact, I had the whole area to myself."

"So?" said Jolson. "Let's make sure we share the sport this very afternoon then. To make it even more interesting we can wager on bull's-eyes."

"Excellent," said Ambassador Kimbrough.

The heavy mist rolled in between them and the big straw-backed target. Jolson could still make out the trio of many branched trees off to the left. He touched briefly with his elbow the truth kit, now taped under his blue sweatunic. "Am I correct in assuming," he said to the ambassador, "the sport of archery comes to us from some remote region of the Terra System, one of the Earth planets?"

Kimbrough's bow twanged and an arrow disappeared into the deepening fog. "Wait now, Gabney. I want to hear the thunk."

While they waited for the sound of the arrow sinking into the nearstraw of the now invisible target Jolson forked his hand under his blue tunic and eased a small flask from the truth kit. "There," he said.

"You heard it strike?"

"Sounded to be a dead-center hit, to these old ears." The mist was swirling thicker and Jolson stepped nearer Kimbrough. "Perhaps a little something to warm the bones, Kimbrough?"

"Not a bad notion," said the ambassador, reaching for the flask. "What is it?"

"Brandy from Peregrine."

"Well," said Kimbrough, uncapping the small container, "exactly what I'm in the mood for, Gabney." He drank. "You?"

Jolson ran the nock of his arrow along his front teeth. "I carry it only for friends, Kimbrough." He retrieved the flask, slipped it away.

"Yes," said Kimbrough, "archery comes to us from Earth itself. Well, it's your turn at the target."

Jolson fitted an arrow to his bowstring, frowned into the heavy gray mist. He sent off an arrow, waited. "Not the best conditions for archery, Kimbrough, even for two lovers of the sport such as ourselves."

Kimbrough cleared his throat and lowered his bow. "You know, Gabney, when I was a boy I went to school on the planet Earth and was, in fact, second in my class at John Foster Dulles Academy." He widened his eyes, coughed again. "I really feel I must tell you something, Gabney. This is a secret, a secret known to few if any of even my closest friends and associates. But, Gabney, I must inform you that when I was eleven years old I paid Norman L. Hilts ten dollars to write my thesis on late-twentieth-century billboards. The grading computer in that particular course, Highway Beautification Two-B, never cared much for me, Gabney. It sensed I didn't like it much, big ugly green thing. The kind we had then. You can hate a computer, Gabney, but you can't love it. Computer sensed that. Which is why I paid Norman L. Hilts the ten dollars."

Jolson caught the ambassador by the arm and headed him for the trees. "Fine, but what about Group A? What can you tell me about an organization called Group A?"

"When I was thirteen I kissed Estelle Banderman in the appliance complex of her grandmother's senior city tower. That happens to be the absolute truth, Gabney."

"I appreciate your confiding in me," said Jolson.

"I wish you'd address me as Mr. Ambassador. I really don't like all the chummy stuff they go for around here."

"That's understandable," said Jolson. "Now what do you know about Group A, about the disappearance of Dean Swift?"

The misty wind rattled the dry leaves and branches. "Here's another true fact," said Kimbrough, his eyes struggling to focus on Jolson. "I really did swipe that dictadesk on Barafunda. At the official hearing I said I'd never seen the thing. Not so, Gabney. All along it was on my vacation satellite off Peregrine, along with the secretary who operated it."

Jolson said, "What do you know about who's taking members of the War Bureau, Mr. Ambassador?" Jolson hesitated. The truth drug in the brandy wasn't taking strong-enough hold. He got out the truth kit, selected a syringe and gave the ambassador an injection of a more powerful drug.

Kimbrough's dusky face paled. He swayed and said, "Those testimonial dinners on Barnum, Gabney. I took all the cash and bought a solar-powered motel on Murdstone. When the sun shines the whole thing spins like a merry-go-round. Tourists seem to like it. Had another motel on Peregrine but it went down a palisade during a mudstorm. We refunded the rent to everybody we could find afterwards." He back-stepped until he was braced by a tree trunk.

"Swift. Dean Swift, Admiral Rockisle, General Moosman. What do you know about them?"

"Well," said the ambassador, "yes, I passed on the information. Naturally I'm privy to the comings and goings of the War Bureau."

Jolson leaned closer. The Political Espionage Office had been right. "Who do you pass your information on to?"

"Encode it first, relay it across the city, Esperanza City. From my office to there."

"Where, to who?"

"He's a very likable young man. Doesn't call me Mr. Ambassador as often as I'd like but he's basically a friendly, outgoing young fellow."

"Give me his name."

"His name," said Kimbrough, his voice hoarse, "is

Robert Leslie Rover. He's prominent in civic affairs and the manager of Esperanza City's most popular funspire. And he was, if memory serves, runner-up for the title of Esperanza Man of the Year last year."

"Okay," said Jolson. "Why are you doing all this?"

Kimbrough was breathing fast, rocking. "It's Earth, Gabney."

"What?"

"Earth supreme. Someday they say Earth will be supreme, in all the systems."

"Is Rover running the whole operation?"

"No, A is. Group A. No, Robert Leslie Rover is merely an employee, I'm sure. A likable-enough young man, thoroughly outgoing, but not leader material."

"Who do you think does head up Group A?" Jolson asked.

"Not the faintest notion do I have. I simply pass my information along, to Rover. On one occasion I assisted him in getting Admiral Rockisle out of his hotel and into the funspire. It's not really for the idea of Earth supremacy that I'm doing it exactly, Gabney, though you're always loyal to the planet whereon you receive your early schooling. No, it's mostly for the fee Group A gives me, Gabney, a generous fee. I do what they ask, restrain my curiosity. Being in public life can be extremely costly."

"Do you know where Group A has its headquarters?"

"No," said Kimbrough. "Speaking of Group A, though, you might want to know this." He shivered, straightened, his eyelids fluttering.

"Yeah, go on."

"I'm not used to that uncut Peregrine stuff these days," said the ambassador. He felt the tree at his back. "Quite a jolt, Gabney. Thanks for propping me up. Did I actually pass out?"

"Only for an instant, Kimbrough."

"No recollection of it," said Kimbrough. "Don't mention this episode to Franklin T. Tripp. He'd get the information fed into my medigroup computer back in Esperanza City. That computer really has it in for me. Ever notice, Gabney, you can hate a computer but you can't love one."

Jolson said, "The rec period must be about over. Shall we head in?"

"One thing first," said the ambassador.

"Yes?"

"I want to go take a look and see if our arrows hit the target." He chuckled and Jolson led him into the mist.

EIGHT

FLEXING first, Nat Hockering wheeled the hair dryer across the neartile floor of the quiet blue cubicle. "Exercise can only do so much, Mr. Gabney," he said. He parked the dryer, scratched at his jaw with hooked fingers. "The same goes for intelligent dieting. They're all important, but for really chopping away the years you still have to fall back on cosmetic aids."

Jolson was tilted way back in a medical feeling chair, his head under a faucet and over a basin. "How much is it going to cost me, Hockering?"

"Don't let my grumpiness last night set you off your stride, Mr. Gabney." Hockering ground his large hands together, laughing deep in his chest. "In the daylight and early evening hours I'm generally pretty affable." He speared a roped bar of Nepenthe-labeled soap and began massaging Jolson's thin white hair, forcing his head further back. "I used to work for one of the larger embalming outfits in Esperanza City, until I found that too damned frustrating. You just get somebody looking pretty good and they bury him. This way I can admire my stuff afoot for a while."

"Ease up a little," said Jolson. "My old bones are a bit strained in this awkward position."

"When I get myself established in the architecture field," said the wide attendant, "I'll probably drop the cosmetics thing altogether. There's a falseness to it all." He rested one hand lightly on Jolson's throat. "Hey, I want to tell you something."

Jolson strained to swing upright. "Oh, so?"

"Think about this. Fingerprints."

Jolson tensed. "What's that, Hockering?"

"You screwed up. You look like old Leonard F. Gabney, you even sort of act like him, but you don't have his fingerprints." Hockering's thick fingers tightened below Jolson's Adam's apple. "It's always the little details that foul us up. See, we got a man with a tap on the Political Espionage Office's Barnum headquarters, a tap on their main dispozhole. That got us a look at a triplicate of a memo requesting a Chameleon Corps guy to head out to Esperanza and dig into the War Bureau snatches. We've been on guard since, screening people who came here. We figured PEO might have something on Kimbrough."

Jolson gagged. "Tripp in this, too?"

"The two of us, yeah. Plus old Kimbrough himself. With him it's not a question of belief, it's dough." Hockering grunted and brought up his free hand to fend off Jolson's clutching hands. "I'm going to strangle you now. We'll sink you in the mud pool for a while and then make up a cover story about what happened to you. That mud should be very good for your complexion."

Jolson concentrated. His neck grew some and stretched six inches, thinning away from Hockering's heavy grip. Jolson elongated his fingers and jabbed them into the heavy man's eyes. There were certain advantages to having been processed by the Chameleon Corps. Jolson shrunk down a foot in size, knifed out of the chair.

"Jolson," said Hockering, knuckling his reddening eyes.

"Jolson of the Chameleon Corps. That's who you are. Not too far from now you'll be a body in the mud."

Jolson got his balance against the hair dryer. He picked up the nearmetal pole and swung the whole thing at the charging Hockering.

Hockering bobbed, dodged the whistling blow. The headpiece of the dryer dominoed a dozen squeeze bottles off a shelf just above Hockering. Wrinkle eraser, crowfoot retarder, underarm purifier, afterplunge lotion, pastoral cologne, realleather aroma, others. They bounced to the floor, splashing, squirting, hissing.

"Take it easy, Jolson. I got the responsibility of keeping this hole tidy." Hockering leaped.

Jolson walked sideways. His sandal slid, lubricated by a snake of hair restoring cream on the floor. Jolson fell.

Hockering sat down on him hard, grabbing again for his throat.

Pistoning with his elbows Jolson somersaulted the heavy Hockering off. While Hockering untangled himself from perfumes and scents Jolson rose up and retrieved the hair dryer. He swung it again and caught Hockering full on the point of his chin.

The big man flapped up, spun and tumbled toward the sink. His already damaged chin smacked the basin edge and he wiped down the wall, his spread fingers rubbing small circles on the pale mosaic squares. He reached the floor unconscious.

Jolson, listening, frowned at his own finger tips. After a long minute he stepped out of the cosmetic treatment room, first cleaning most of the signs of struggle off his blue sweatsuit. He moved calmly, mingling with the few old men in the corridor.

He found his way to an exit ramp and turned down it, aiming at one of the landcruiser parking areas he'd seen earlier in the day.

"A word with you, sir," called Wing Commander Eberhardt, who stepped suddenly out of a room marked SOUVENIRS FOR GRANDCHILDREN IN THE 6 TO 8 GROUP.

"Wing Commander?" said Jolson, not slowing.

"I've been brooding about our deforestation of California, Oregon and that other state. How do you feel about it, sir?"

"Wing Commander," said Jolson, "I find myself in complete disagreement with your overblown and, may I add, cockeyed and pigheaded opinions."

"Why, you old geezer," said the Wing Commander.

"I'm stepping out into that landcruiser parking area," said Jolson. "If you have any honor, which seems dubious, I advise you to gather up some dueling gear and meet me there before darkness falls completely. It's time you defended your beastly opinions, you old curmudgeon."

The Wing Commander gave a quick cry. "I accept the challenge, you withered old rascal. I'll meet you in less than a quarter hour."

That got rid of Wing Commander Eberhardt long enough for Jolson to find a landcruiser he could get away in. He increased his pace, pushed out of the main Nepenthe building.

Five cruisers were parked in the twilight lot. The second one Jolson tried was not locked. He half-sat, one-hipped, in the control seat and got to work jobbing the starter panel enough so he could drive the cruiser.

Treads squealed, and through the open-grilled gateway came a gray landcruiser, painted the exact shade of the early night. The car roared closer, the window opened itself and someone called numbers out at Jolson.

"Go away, Jennifer," said Jolson. "I'm trying to make a quiet unobtrusive escape from this place."

"I know," said the girl agent. She had her dark hair pulled back, which heightened her cheekbones. "Get in and we'll elude everybody."

The exit door Jolson had used snapped open and Hockering came weaving onto the nearmacadam. He had a bunched blue jumpsuit pressed against his bleeding chin and a short-barreled blaster rifle in his right hand, braced on his hip. "The hell with cute stuff," he yelled. "I'll fry you where you stand."

Jennifer lowered her window guard five inches further, brought up a hand blaster and fired. Hockering's rifle pinwheeled from his grasp and cracked him hard across the temple. He growled and tumbled backward, sitting. The blue sweatsuit drifted down after him and covered his face.

Jolson ran low and jumped into the gray cruiser, landing next to Jennifer. "Thanks, ma'am."

"I knew you were in trouble because of the apricot." She spun the landcruiser sharply and they shot from the Nepenthe, Inc., lot.

"The what?"

"Apricot, the one with the warning device," the girl said. "You squeezed it."

"Nope, not me," said Jolson. The girl was still wearing the perfume he'd noticed in Esperanza City. "I really didn't send for help, Jennifer."

"I got a warning signal a good couple hours ago," she said. "So I came on out to lend a hand, on whatever was needed. That worked out pretty well with the pistol, huh? Shooting that guy's rifle."

"Yeah," Jolson admitted. "I could probably have hot-wired that other cruiser and gotten off free before he even had a chance to shoot."

"Who was he?"

"Nat Hockering."

"I practice a lot on PEO's secret target range, but in the field I'm not always that good," said the girl. She grinned across at Jolson.

He watched her face for a second, grinned back. "I never did use that apricot, though. Hockering or Tripp must have searched my luggage and activated the thing by accident."

"Why'd they search your luggage, if they did?"

Jolson rubbed his finger tips with his thumbs. "They tumbled I wasn't Gabney, that I was Ben Jolson of the CC."

"Just how?"

Jolson told her just how and about what he'd learned from Ambassador Kimbrough.

"I'll get people checking on Tripp and Hockering," Jennifer said. "Do we want to pick them up yet?"

Jolson shook his head. "I think Hockering knows more than Kimbrough. Can we put a tail on him quick, see where he heads? He's bound to depart Nepenthe now."

"Sure," said Jennifer. She uncorked a dash mike and spoke a paragraph of numbers into it. "PEO has a couple of men hidden out near Nepenthe. I didn't send them in after you, because I wanted to handle it myself."

Jolson said, "The guy Kimbrough reports to, this Robert Leslie Rover, we want to find out more about him."

"I know some already," said the girl agent. "I'll get you more information. The best place to catch him is in that funspire of his. Oh, by the way, I got a memo from Head Mickens of the Political Espionage Office."

"Yeah," said Jolson.

"He said, though not this tersely, you're to go on and pursue any leads you uncover. Adopt any new identities you need. He said if the Kimbrough lead led to anything he was sure he could get an extra grant from someplace. So you can even go over the usual CC budget."

"Kimbrough," said Jolson. "He ought to be quietly taken out of circulation."

Jennifer smiled. "I know, I put that in the code message a minute ago."

Jolson reached over his shoulder and massaged his old man's back. "Good about the extra money. I saved some dough on this Nepenthe thing, by not staying more than two days. I can use it all on Robert Leslie Rover."

Jennifer gunned the cruiser onto the six-level roadway leading to Esperanza City. "Money, yes. A good way to get an edge with him."

Jolson said, "How come this landcar? Wouldn't an air-cruiser have been quicker?"

"Restrictions. No air travel over any of the cemeteries. That way Esperanza can control the tourist end of things better, keep it on the ground. Bigger profit margin."

"Not complaining, just curious," said Jolson. He relaxed back, watched the night growing around them, watched the girl's profile.

"You going to stay an old man for the rest of the trip home, Ben?" she asked, glancing over at him.

"I think I'm too tired to change."

"Do I ever," asked Jennifer, "get to see you as yourself, as Ben Jolson?"

"Afterwards," said Jolson.

NINE

"THAT'S the best funspire," said the naked robot and pointed toward the lavender-tinted wraparound window of the cocktail lounge. "Right across there, sir." The female android arranged Jolson's drink on an ebony coaster.

"Is it the one managed by a guy named Robert Leslie Rover?" he asked. The spire was forty stories high, chrome-colored, glaring now in the last of the day's sunlight. "I've heard his funspire was the one to visit."

The android nodded Yes while wiping moisture off her bare stomach with a black-bordered cocktail napkin. "Mr. Rover comes here to the Top o' the Apex frequently. Despite his being very civic-minded, he's a good sport."

Jolson produced his Apex Hotel chargecard and the android clicked it into the slot in her wrist, returned it. "Is tipping allowed?" asked Jolson.

"It's figured into the price of your drink," said the girl robot. "You can pinch me if you'd like, at no extra charge."

Jolson shrugged. "I'll pass."

"People from different planets have different customs," said the robot. "You're from Peregrine, aren't you, Mr. Gillespie? The computer at the desk told me."

Jolson was tall and blond now, about thirty and with a resort tan. "That's right, miss, and we're somewhat reserved on Peregrine."

The android said, "Mr. Rover never fondles me much

either. He was born right here on Esperanza, too. You meet all kinds." She laughed, turned slowly and walked to the next booth.

Peregrine-made cigarettes used a puckering neartobacco. Jolson lit one taken from his chrome-colored case and leaned back against the black realleather. The gritty yellow haze that blurred the city by day was fading as evening came on. Jolson could see the metallic-faced, glass-rich buildings of Esperanza City more clearly now. Random colored light patterns began to play on the bright surfaces. Rover's funspire was flickering with sharp pastels.

"Is that you?"

Jolson's hand went up and brushed at his short curled blond hair. "Hi, Jennifer. Sit down."

The girl Political Espionage Office agent was wearing a pair of lemon-yellow cocktail slacks and a chambray singlet. "Gilbert Gillespie, huh? The hydroponics heir from Peregrine. You've done a great job with the quick briefing we were able to give you. You got the money PEO sent over, the chargecards, ID packet, fingerprint data?"

"Security, Jennifer," Jolson said softly.

"Oh, PEO finances this saloon," said the slim girl. "We can talk freely."

The naked girl android returned for Jennifer's order. Jolson said, "PEO think up the decor, too?"

Jennifer tilted her head slightly to the left. "The girls have all got mikes built in."

"Rover is supposed to come in here," said Jolson after the android had clicked Jennifer's brandy down on its dark coaster. "Has your bug network picked up anything?"

"He wears a counter-bug, as do most people around here. Still we get something interesting every now and then."

From a hip bag she took a red-covered diary. "I wrote out a report on Rover in longhand, since we devoted most of your sleep briefing to getting you backgrounded on Gillespie. This will fill you in and then I'll go along to Rover's funspire with you, to back you on anything unexpected."

Jolson opened the book, his forefinger tapped the first page. "I'm going to go in alone, Jennifer," he said, glancing at the spire. "Later on tonight."

Jennifer made a humming. "Okay, Ben. PEO says I have to cooperate. I feel a playboy should have a girl along, at least as a prop."

"What's this first line say?"

Jennifer put her hand on his, turning the page so she could read it. "His name. Rover, Robert Leslie, age forty-two."

"Your handwriting is half printing," said Jolson. "You also get the lower case and the upper case mixed."

Jennifer retrieved the book. "I'll read it to you, Ben." She ran her tongue along her lower lip. "I know why you're being critical. You're trying to discourage me, to keep me from taking the play away from you. I am pretty competent."

Jolson said, "Tell me about Rover."

"He's forty-two, about five and a half feet tall. He's square-jawed and sort of obviously handsome, except he looks like somebody took a six-foot-tall man and scrunched him down to Rover. He's assistant chairman of the Junior Chamber of Commerce, as well as manager of the funspire. As I told you before, it's commonly accepted that the organized crime cartel in the Barnum System runs most of the funspires. Meaning Robert Leslie Rover has to be tied in with the organization, though no one has proved it." She folded her hands over the open pages. "The PEO files are full of vague references about someone named Alberto."

"A syndicate man?"

"Yes," said Jennifer. "He's supposed to have one whole floor of Rover's funspire to himself and to be very difficult to meet. We think he's masterminding most of the rackets on Esperanza. Money seems to come in to him and it's fairly certain he takes a large cut of the funspire profits. He doesn't seem to have been mentioned in connection with Group A, though."

"What does the Interplanet Justice Society say about Alberto?"

The girl said, "IJS can't get anything positive on Alberto and we're sure they've lost at least two agents in Rover's spire. That's what our men inside IJS tell us."

Jolson lifted his glass. "The Political Espionage Office has infiltrated the Justice Society, too?"

"Sure," said Jennifer. "You know, I didn't actually plan to work for PEO at all. When I was in college I was assistant president of the Student Aid to Underfed Planets Committee."

"Was that about the time the stories about its being a PEO front broke?"

"Right, Ben. I didn't like the idea of being duped. I quit and joined the Student Peace Group."

Jolson nodded. "A mistake again. PEO has been fifty per cent of SPG since the last war."

"I found that out," said Jennifer. She smiled quickly. "After college I went to work for the Birth Control and Minimum Food Aid Society. Well, you know what came out about them."

"Yeah, PEO was financing all their out-of-the-Barnum-

System activities, using the reps to gather counterinsurgency stuff."

Jennifer said, "When I switched to the Institute for the Study of Remote Planets I thought I could settle down finally, in a job I really liked."

After sipping his drink, Jolson said, "I remember when the Barnum Educational Network broke that story. A reporter named Sol S. Mahones dug it up. The IFTSORP was a straight PEO cover group."

"Yes," said Jennifer. "That's when I gave up. I got a job with PEO itself and now, for the first time, I know who I'm actually working for. Makes things a lot easier, in some ways."

Jolson laughed. "Reluctance is a good thing sometimes."

"Not in a Chameleon Corps man?"

Jolson turned to watch the funspire, bright now against the night. "Anything else in there about Rover?"

"His funspire is one of the few places PEO hasn't been able to plant a permanent agent," said Jennifer. "Rover has a good defense system."

In front of a booth across the dim room a naked girl android said, "Ouch." Standing next to her on the thick sable rug was a pink shaggy man whose thick arms were bobbing loosely. He chuckled, his flat nose wrinkling. Then he did a full reverse somersault and pinched the android again just under the left buttock. "Ouch," she repeated.

"That's Mayor Kriegspiel," said Jennifer. She closed the diary. "Albert 'Dub' Kriegspiel."

"I understand the grab but not the backflip."

"He used to be a television acrobat before he got into politics."

Kriegspiel giggled, wagged his wide head and squeezed into the booth. "Earth whiskey," he told the girl android.

"Kriegspiel's on the take, too," said Jennifer.

"Hard to believe."

The flower urn on the mayor's table quivered slightly. Kriegspiel's elbows swung to rest on the table top. He grimaced at the urn, then yanked it up. An urn-colored metal disc fell clear.

"One of your bugging devices?" asked Jolson.

Jennifer stroked her cheek. "No, we don't use those bulky ones any more."

The mayor jumped wide-footed to the thick rug and cartwheeled his heavy table out of its place. Underneath a small-faced man with straight dark hair was hunched. "I have a policy of no interviews," shouted Mayor Kriegspiel. "Especially with muckrakes." He plucked the thin eaves-dropper up and adjusted him on his back like a cloak.

"That looks like Sol S. Mahones," said Jennifer, half rising. "The educational network reporter."

Jolson was free of their booth and moving for the mayor, who had the reporter spinning rapidly on his shoulders now. "Home on Peregrine," said Jolson, "we don't much care for senseless violence, sir."

Mayor Kriegspiel grinned, wiggled his head, kept Mahones spinning. "Are you aware, cousin, who I am?"

"More important," said Jolson as he grabbed the mayor's nearest arm hard above the elbow, "do you know me?"

Kriegspiel slowed the reporter some, scowled at Jolson. "You seem to be Gilbert Gillespie, the hydroponics heir. Until now you've never visited our little planet and I must say I'm happy to have you here." He straightened and Mahones slid off and into a standing position. "I hope I haven't offended you with this piece of innocent cutting up."

"On Peregrine," said Jolson, "we place great faith in dignity."

The mayor said, "As we do here. My. I don't know why I'm not out lifting weights and doing a few fast laps around one of our beautiful free indoor parks. That's the dignified way to work off high spirits, isn't it? Mention me to your father, Gillespie." The mayor grinned, wiggled, and hurried away across the black rugs.

Sol S. Mahones held out his hand to Jolson. "Thanks, Gillespie," he said. "I'm trying to put together a three-part documentary on civic corruption on Esperanza."

Shaking hands, Jolson said, "Your listening equipment's too big."

"The budget," said the reporter. He retrieved his bug and a palm size video camera from the hollow left by Mayor Kriegspiel's flung table. "Your saving me from harm is something of a problem for me, Gillespie."

"How?"

"I've got a lot of good material about the corrupt practices of your own family that I've been thinking of using in a later series."

"Well, now on my home planet of Peregrine," began Jolson.

"Never mind," Mahones said. "My conscience is in control again. But thanks."

With Jennifer, Jolson said, "Hydroponics can really cushion you."

"You could have handled it as Ben Jolson," said the girl. "Hey, speaking of which, how did you get into the Chameleon Corps, Ben?"

"I promised Mahones an exclusive on the story," said Jolson. "Another drink?"

Jennifer said, "No, I'm leaving. Good luck on your mission." She left.

"A shame," said his robot waitress. "Maybe if you pinched me a couple times you'd be better able to accept your girl leaving you so abruptly."

"No," said Jolson.

TEN

T H E vendor of black balloons hissed at Jolson.

Halting on the marbled sidewalk in front of Robert Leslie Rover's funspire, Jolson said, "Beg pardon?" to the narrow-bearded man.

The street vendor waited until two men in silver evening suits passed inside. Then he said, "15–6–1–24–26–9–6."

"You guys have no sense of privacy. What is it?"

One of the PEO undercover man's souvenir balloons, inscribed "Death hath ten thousand several doors," flew loose of his grasp and drifted away and upward. The vendor said, "Hockering's inside. We spotted him going in, about an hour ago."

"I had a different face at Nepenthe, Inc.," said Jolson. His laminated frock coat was bothering him around the shoulders. He shifted and added, "I'll just go on in, as planned."

"Wait for the whole message, will you?" The Political Espionage man paused while a group of wide men in gold-buttoned suits hustled into the funspire lobby, each carrying a large floral wreath. "Jennifer will meet you on the gaming floor."

"Jennifer's in there?" asked Jolson. "Damn it, Hockering knows about her. He must have got a look at her when she picked me up out at Nepenthe."

"She told me you had the habit of down-playing our

abilities," said the vendor. "Of course she took precautions in order not to be recognized."

"What exactly?"

"She's got a blonde wig on. When you get up to Floor Thirteen, which is where Rover spends most of his time, Jennifer will contact you."

"What's she doing here?"

"Hockering's presence is likely to complicate the situation. Jennifer decided to take a direct hand, to back your play."

Jolson rubbed the left side of his playboy face. "How long she been here?"

"Fifteen minutes."

Another heavy wreath went by and Jolson asked the PEO man, "What are all the flowers for?"

"One of Alberto's henchmen passed away, a guy named Socks Rubion. They're holding a wake on the top floor, Alberto's floor."

Jolson got out a dollar. "Sell me a balloon, in case we're being watched."

"Oh, good idea, good cover dodge." He gave Jolson a balloon with the inscription "Death borders upon our birth."

The funspire lobby was thick with fountains and invisible music, loud and electronic. A platinum-haired girl dressed in gilt stars accidentally popped Jolson's balloon with her pipe. Before she could apologize the sway and motion of the other fifty people in the lobby carried her toward the row of elevators.

Jolson's elbow became hooked with a red and gold wreath that had "Death be not proud" in script on its scarlet ribbon.

"Show some respect," said the rumble-voiced man carrying the piece.

"Sorry," said Jolson. "Back on my home planet of Peregrine we separate our pleasures from our mourning."

"You mess any more with my flowers and I'll knock you on your ass."

Jolson untangled his arm, scattering a few crimson petals, and worked himself to a different stretch of lobby. He came up flush with a gold-doored elevator that went to Floors Ten through Fifteen.

Another gangster with a wreath was inside the packed elevator cabinet. "I'm in the wrong car," he told Jolson. "I can feel the blossoms withering while I delay."

Jolson twisted and read the wreath. "Death will have his day."

"By the time I got to my neighborhood flower shop all the good sentiments were gone."

Except for the gangman with the wreath, all the passengers left the elevator at Floor Thirteen. There were several hundred people already in the vast, many-leveled gambling room. Jolson lit one of his terrible Peregrine cigarettes and went down a soft ramp to the bingo tables.

An elderly spotted woman shot up from the ornate table nearest Jolson and cried out, "Bingo."

The white-clothed game manager lowered rimless spectacles from his perspiring forehead to his eyes and squinted at the woman's card. He shook his head negatively. The freckled matron swung a loose fist at him and two white-suited bouncers came running. They got a complex armlock on her and rushed her to the elevators.

Beyond the bingo area two dozen people ringed a round white table. The game manager here was raising an antique filigreed pistol toward his head. "Empty or loaded?" he asked the group.

"Empty," said a pretty, rapid-breathing brunette. "Five thousand says it's empty."

"Loaded, ten thousand," said a Territorial Commando Colonel in a dress green uniform.

"I'll match you," returned the dark girl.

"All bets down?" said the man with the pistol. After a beat he squeezed the trigger. There was an explosion and the side of his head blew away. Gears and cogwheels jingled and clattered, splashing the slick white table top and the bettors.

The bouncers hurried over and hauled the ruined android away, replacing him with a short, fatter robot. "Empty or loaded?" the android asked and picked up the pistol.

Jolson wandered by blackjack, whist, roulette, bolasete, Monopoly, liar's dice, lotto, Earth poker, embotada, Venusian keno, cooncan, Barnum craps and seven tables of computer logic games. He was certain he'd know Jennifer, that quirky smile and the sharp cheekbones, even though she was disguised with a blonde wig. But there was no sign of her.

Turning away from a bank of creditplate slot machines, Jolson walked into the hard elbow of Nat Hockering. "Oops," said Jolson.

The Nepenthe, Inc., attendant was wearing a black near-leather tail coat with rhinestone floral patterns on its back and sides. "Hey now," said Hockering. Five blue vinyl jackstones leaped out of his palm and sank into the rug. He grunted at Jolson. "You outlanders are pretty clumsy."

"Please forgive me," said Jolson. "On my home planet of

Peregrine we always apologize, whether we are at fault or no."

Hockering studied Jolson's present face for a few seconds. He bent and scooped up the fallen jackstones and spun around to resume his game.

Jolson smiled at Hockering's jeweled back and began another slow circle of the gaming floor. The short fat android's head got shot off as he repassed that section. Jolson jumped sideways to avoid a swarm of tiny silver nuts and bolts mingled with finespun wires.

He straightened, reached into a laminated pocket for his cigarette case.

A large hand closed on his arm. "Terrific," said a grinning voice. "Just who I'm looking for."

ELEVEN

STILL holding tight to Jolson's arm, the taut, compact man said, "Hello, I'm Bob Rover. You're looking swell, Gil."

Jolson held out his hand and Rover let go and shook it. "I'm Gilbert Gillespie, home-based on Peregrine."

Rover had a deep even tan and rippling hair. He smiled, involving all the muscles in his strong-jawed face. "I know, I've seen pictures, heard all about you, Gil. Quite the playboy, right? It's terrific having you aboard. I wish you'd made an advance reservation so I could have planned something a little more marvelous."

"On my home planet we act on impulse a lot," said Jolson. He glanced around Rover, still hoping to find Jennifer.

"I've got a terrific notion, Gil." Rover punched Jolson in the side. "I'm going to give you the guided tour, show you around my spire. From what I've been told I figure you've got other interests than gambling."

"I'd appreciate a look around, Bob."

"Hold it a second." Rover made a running leap, just in time to tackle the freckled old woman with the grudge against the bingo area. She had come charging out of the stairwell with a brand new hand pistol. The bouncers bulldogged her and Rover hopped up and back to Jolson. "Come on over this way. I have a swell private elevator.

Some guys from the Junior Chamber of Commerce had it built for me. Sleeps four and has a private bar."

Rover helped Jolson cinch his white surgical gown. "Hey, I'm really sorry you didn't like the drug floor," Rover said. "Or even our Gluttony Pavilion."

"I ate before I came over," said Jolson.

They were on Floor Sixteen, in a silent gray corridor. An android nurse appeared from around a dim corner. The unconscious man on the wheeled table she was pushing moaned. The front of the nurse's tunic was splashed with blood.

"Pretty terrific, right?" said Rover, nudging Jolson above the kidneys.

The patient groaned once more before he was wheeled away into another gray corridor.

"Very authentic-looking," said Jolson.

Rover raised his white face mask up and covered his smiling mouth. "We use real blood. The customers prefer it, as I don't have to tell you." He gripped Jolson and pulled him along. "Where to first, Gil? We're pretty lucky tonight, with a real operation to watch over in Surgery. Something to do with a growth in the stomach, a real antique disease. We had to teleport the patient and the physician in from the back country of Murdstone."

"I'm not," said Jolson, "in the mood for watching much surgery tonight."

"I'm glad everybody isn't feeling like you. We get five hundred people here on Floor Sixteen every evening, and it's not seasonal like free-fall hockey or dwarf basketball."

"Five hundred people pay to watch operations?"

"Isn't all surgery," explained Rover. He yanked Jolson

through a door labeled Incurable Wing. "Here's our newest concession. Really terrific, does marvelous business. I'm not at liberty to quote you specific figures, but it's a heck of a money-maker."

This corridor was painted a dull pale brown. Through an open door a fat man showed on a stiff bed. Wires and tubes were attached up and down his almost white body. "He's paying you for this, too?"

"Sure." Rover laughed. "It's the old incurable-disease dodge. You know how great it feels to get over an illness. You're positive you're cashing in, then they come along and save you, snatch you back from the brink, the jaws. You feel terrific and better than ever. You can't make a recovery, though, if you can't get sick. For a fee folks can come in and get an old-fashioned disease, one that looks sure to kill them off good. They suffer like crazy for a few hours, how much they suffer depending on how much they pay. We step in and cure them. They feel really terrific. In our Barnum System, what with the Universal Health Organization and all, it's no easy thing to get a really frightening disease any more."

From a distance came a quick female scream. "Somebody suffering?" asked Jolson.

"No," said Rover, his mask bobbing with amusement, "what you heard is coming from our Nurses' Dorm area. We get a lot of customers who like to sleep with hospital personnel. Live personnel, which you'll still find in some of the sticks planets. Only time these guys are happy is when they're knocking off a little on the sly with a nurse. That's not always easy to arrange on your home planet. We have a really terrific assortment of nurses, too. Hey, the great part is, they are actually nurses. Yeah, and even have med school diplomas stuck up on the walls of their rooms. Those little details, Gil, are what make a place better than just great. The edge, what you get from paying attention to little details is the edge over the other guy." He ground his fist against Jolson's ear in a friendly way. "Now, what disease are you in the market for?"

Jolson puckered his left cheek. "I don't know, Bob. I'm already getting a headache. I don't like to fool with disease when I'm not feeling well."

Rover forked down his mask to let Jolson see his pout. "Say, Gil, what's wrong with you? We've heard about you, carrying on on Peregrine. You're supposed to be a real terrific hospital buff. I read a gossip column said you liked to vacation in the Isolation Ward of the Gillespie Memorial Hospital once a year. I had a real terrific malady set aside just for you, Gil. A plague. A real one and not some government weapon thing. Ours starts off with you getting bitten by this swell creepy insect. You sure you're not up to it?"

Jolson said, "I'm going to be around Esperanza for a while, Bob. Reserve the plague for my next visit."

"You'll have to put a deposit."

Jolson handed over his chargecard. "Okay," he said. His short sleep briefing on Gillespie hadn't mentioned his medical interest.

"Hey, I know something else about you," said Rover as he clicked the card into a pocket register and then returned it. "We'll go right on up to Floor Twenty, skip the Violence Park and the Bullfight floor. We'll express ourselves to Twenty, which I know you're going to be in the mood for, Gil."

"Twenty?"

Rover took off his mask. "Girls."

By himself in the narrow pink room, Jolson watched the man-size computer in front of him. The pink machine had garlands of crisp white lace and was dotted with red enamel hearts. "This method, honey," said the machine in a burred maternal voice, "makes sure there's no mistakes and everybody is happy."

Jolson lit an awful cigarette and grinned his Gillespie grin. "Terrific," he said.

The machine whirred. "Now, toots, you fill out the forms and carefully list all your preferences in femaledom. Oh, listen, sweetie, it is girls you're interested in, isn't it? You look straight to me, but you can imagine we get all kinds here."

"Girls, yes."

"I figured you weren't like that, honey." A punch form clicked out of the machine and Jolson caught it. "I even had a couple guys, botanists from Murdstone, make a pass at me."

"You're pretty attractive," said Jolson, "for a computer."

"I take care of myself," answered the machine. "Why kid myself, though, nobody can really love a computer."

"So I've heard." After he'd filled out the preference and personality forms Jolson slipped them in a slot in the machine's left side. "I put two alternate choices."

"Good, tootsie, that'll speed up service."

The machine purred for nearly two minutes. "Funny," it said finally. "We didn't have you figured this way at all, Gillespie. We had a really plump little blonde, with sweet plump knees, in mind for you. But if it's rangy brunettes you seem to want tonight, it's rangy brunettes you'll get. We aim to please. Exit by door G-Four, sweetie."

Five burly men in leather vests and rough trousers were sitting about a realwood table, toasting each other with giant tankards of green ale. "Welcome to the Fox and Hounds Inn, stranger," said the nearest.

They all laughed in welcome and another called to Jolson, "Quaff with us, stranger."

Jolson studied the smoky room he'd stepped into, its beamed ceiling and deep real fireplace. "I'd be pleased to," he said. "On my home planet we never turn down an opportunity to quaff, though that's not what I'm here for exactly."

He crossed to a long realwood bar and stopped by a bronze fox-headed ale spigot. A slim brunette girl appeared from a back room and slipped her hand up onto the spigot handle, smiling across the bar at Jolson. "Do they bother you?" she asked.

"Androids, aren't they?"

"Yes," said the girl. "Shall I turn them off?"

"Why don't you."

The dark girl had long slender hands. She extended one. "The usual fee for quiet is ten dollars. You have your chargecard?"

Jolson drew it out. "Right here, ma'am."

The tankards came to rest and the men froze into silence. The girl said, "My room is upstairs here. It's the best room in the Fox and Hounds. Unless you'd prefer right here, on the authentic animal furs before the fire?"

"How much extra for the room?"

"Twenty-five."

"On my home planet of Peregrine we always say you might as well go first-class."

"You've probably heard of the Fox and Hounds even

on Peregrine," said the girl, fitting his card into her pocket register.

"It's famous, as is Mr. Rover's funspire."

"You'll probably want, then, a souvenir menu to take home?"

"Put it on my bill."

"I imagine you smoke," said the girl. "Want a souvenir Fox and Hounds ashtray, too?"

"First-class," said Jolson. "Throw it all in."

With an elbow on the bar, the girl asked, "Do you sleep in pajamas, nightshirt or shift?"

"Might as well get one of each," said Jolson.

"Good," said the girl. "That way you get a discount. They all come with the famous Fox and Hounds symbol on them."

"To save time," said Jolson, "just put me down for everything."

"We can get to bed then, Gil."

"What's your name, by the way?"

"That's up to you," she said. "What would you like to call me?"

"Any difference in price?"

"No."

"You pick it then."

"How about Jennifer?"

Jolson swallowed, frowned. "No," he said slowly, "that's not a favorite of mine. Let's make it Helga."

"Helga it is." The brunette smiled again. "When you said everything, did you want to include the official Fox and Hounds bed sheets and linen?"

"What else," said Jolson.

Robert Leslie Rover gestured with the fried bird wing, wiped his grinning mouth with a fringed napkin and said loudly, "I know this isn't exactly your style, Gil. But Floor Twenty-four makes a terrific breather, a break between the more interesting stuff. Right?"

Jolson and the funspire manager were in a simulated outdoor area: clear pale blue afternoon sky, fields of high yellow grass, bright birds circling far up. Several dozen long tables, each covered with worn checkered covers, surrounded them. A hundred customers were eating a picnic lunch and singing sentimental and patriotic Barnum System ballads.

"This floor does well, too?" asked Jolson.

"Complicated vices, simple virtues," said Rover.

"Mind if we move on?" Jolson stood. There was still no trace of Jennifer and the use of her name by the Fox and Hounds girl was bothering him.

"One more chorus of this song," said Rover. He beat time on his realpaper plate with the crisp wing.

The antique steam roller smashed the flimsy building with much noise and the audience applauded. Fifty muscular men ran into the arena and began attacking the hard rock flooring with nuclear jackhammers. At the other end of the large amphitheater two huge bulldozers and a pile driver, hooked to an eight-speaker amplifier system, ripped up a marble patio. The crowd leaped up, spun hand noise-makers, yelled.

"They never tire of this one," Rover yelled at Jolson's ear. "Our Thirtieth Floor is a really terrific draw, Gil. See, noise shows are still popular on Esperanza, even though they went out of fashion on Barnum itself a good decade ago. We get a lot of folks who are nostalgic about noise."

"What I had in mind—" began Jolson.

"Not another girl?" Rover laughed, rubbing his knuckles on Jolson's short blond hair. "You're terrific, Gil."

"Not more girls," said Jolson. "No, I was thinking about something quieter than this, and competitive." Enough time had been wasted on this tour. He had to find out what Rover knew about Group A, and where Jennifer was. "Sports, Bob. The participant kind."

Rover rocked sideways and clapped his hands. "Wonderful, Gil. Hey, I've got a great notion. Something really swell. We'll buzz up to Floor Thirty-five. I can fix it so we have the whole layout to ourselves, exclusively."

"And Thirty-five is?"

"A really marvelous jungle, Gil," said Rover. "You and I will have ourselves a genuine big game hunt. You'll enjoy the swell wild creatures we have abounding there, teleported from the wilds of all over. Terrific fun. Man stuff."

"Good," said Jolson. As they left their bleacher seats the bulldozers attacked the pile driver.

TWELVE

THE elevator halted a foot above the floor level on Thirty-five and Jolson and Rover had to jump down to the high sharp grass. A few yards across a clearing was a peaked-roof hunting lodge. Stretching enormously away from the rough-hewn lodge was a jungle, shimmering in hot midday glare.

"Pretty sensational, isn't it?" said Rover. He undid his neckpiece and flapped out of his formal coat. "This is a real man's floor, Gil. Fang and claw."

"Always this hot?"

"Matter of fact, the thermostat is a little on the fritz. I could stand it ten degrees cooler and still get the steamy wilderness effect."

Something roared nearby. "What's that?" asked Jolson as he unseamed his laminated jacket.

"That's really terrific, Gil," said Rover. "It's so special we keep it caged up right outside the lodge. So all the customers can get a look, even though most of them can't afford a chance at hunting it."

They rounded the corner of the rustic lodge and Rover grinned and pointed at a massive silvered cage. Jolson said, "Not even from the Barnum System, huh?"

The big animal was a muddy yellow, supple. "We tele-ported the damn thing," explained Rover, waggling a hand at the animal. "They call it a lion, Gil. Isn't it great? A terrific attention-getter and mean as heck. A lion, yeah. Comes all the way from Earth in the Earth System."

"How much would it cost to hunt him?"

Rover bounded up the nearwood steps of the lodge. "Five thousand per half hour, Gil. Don't bother with the lion, we've got something else in mind. Come on in and we'll get into some jungle hunting gear."

The main room's walls were thick with mounted animal heads and the floor was almost hidden by scattered animal-skin rugs.

Rover took off his opera pumps and ground his toes into a thick spotted pelt. "This fellow's extinct now. We got the last one from the back country of Peregrine. Sold the right to clonk him to a banana exporter from Callisto." Dropping down into a hide-and-tubing chair Rover said, "Last night we had a terrific time shooting tharks with a bow and arrow. The only trouble about tharks is they're so slow-footed and dull that you can't be sure sometimes if they're dead or alive. Hit them with an arrow, though, they usually yelp. You at least can tell you've got a hit. Ever hunt much with a bow and arrow, Gil?"

"Back on my home planet of Peregrine," said Jolson. Two suits of buff-colored jungle jump clothes were sprawled out on a fuzzy orange rug. He picked the one nearest his present size and got into it.

"In the next room we have a whole microfilm library with full-color pictures of our entire stock of animals." Rover dropped his formal pants. "Customers can order what they want by numbers and the creature's let loose electronically from its pen out in the jungle. About ninety per cent of our animals are real, which I think is a terrific percentage. We throw in ten per cent android animals because some of our customers seem to like them."

Jolson sealed his tunic. "I'm anxious to browse through your stock."

Rover hurried into his hunting clothes. "Gil, I have a terribly great surprise for you."

The far door swung in and Nat Hockering, wearing a jungle hunting suit, entered and stopped in the center of a scarlet striped skin. "Good to see you again, Chameleon Corps."

"Beg pardon?" said Jolson.

"I was reading an article by that Sol S. Mahones in an exposé monthly," said Hockering. "He pointed out how clumsy the Political Espionage Office can be." Hockering cupped his fist with his palm. "Sending that Jennifer Hark in here in a wig, for God's sake."

Jolson looked to Rover. "I'm afraid I don't understand all this, Bob. Are we going to hunt or listen to this guy?"

"Jolson, we're going to hunt you," Rover grinned. "An idea Hockering got from reading a Murdstone pulp magazine. Myself, I'd simply turn you over to Alberto and let him kill you in one of his quick easy ways."

"We're going to do it my way," said Hockering. "I'm still angry from Nepenthe, Jolson. How this works is, you get a five-minute head start. You run as far into the jungle as you can and then I come after you and kill you."

Rover crossed his legs. "I'm sitting this one out, Jolson. I have to suffer through these hunting parties almost every night as it is. It'll be terrific fun for you and Nat. He's going to hunt you with nothing except a blaster rifle."

"Okay," said Jolson. "Where's Jennifer?"

"Alberto's got her," Hockering said. He bit his thumb knuckle. "Let's proceed, huh?"

"I thought Alberto was having a wake."

Rover said, "Alberto doesn't attend."

Jolson walked toward Hockering. "How'd you get Jennifer to tell you I was inside the funspire and what cover I was using?"

"Easy now." Hockering laughed. "Alberto wouldn't let me run it my way, Jolson. He's gentle compared. Alberto just gives injections. With your PEO girl friend it was tougher because she had a counter truth drug serum in her. Alberto had to use a drug against that. Bob stalled you down on the lower floors while we got all the information out of her we could. Until she wore out."

Jolson backed for the door. Finally he asked, "Is Alberto head of Group A?"

"No," said Rover. "Alberto is strictly organized crime. He's got a wonderful gift for gambling and vice, but he wouldn't come in on Group A. It's a sideline I work at, on my own."

"Move on out into that jungle," ordered Hockering. "Or I'll drop you where you stand."

Jolson nodded, left the lodge. He strode across the high grass, moved into the jungle. It was too hot. He edged the hunters' path and dropped into the brush. The ground was soft and flaky, crumbling slightly as he walked. Bent low, Jolson worked along close to the earth, listening now for the sounds of Hockering.

The jungle was a composite—foliage, trees, flowering shrubs and hanging vines from all the Barnum planets, and from planets Jolson had never seen. Greens, yellows, harsh oranges, flickering reds. Chalky grays, flecked browns. He ducked lower to pass under a swarm of tiny and metallic hovering gnats. The sound effects were turned up high. Directly above him birds from seven planets sang at once, scattering dry leaves. Multiple calls and cries discorded with each other and thunder rolled. A realistic rain, warm and thick, began to fall. Jolson stopped against a sprawling bush heavy with scarlet flowers. Slowly and carefully he started easing back toward the lodge. The rain rattled down through the leaves.

Crouched, eyes narrowed, Jolson risked a survey of the path. Twenty yards up ahead Hockering was on one knee, his stubby fingers massaging a footprint left by Jolson.

Jolson stepped out onto the soggy trail and called to Hockering. "Hey, Nat, come on back. Alberto wants you to call the hunt off." Jolson had Rover's voice and, he hoped, the funspire manager's squat handsome appearance.

Hockering swung around, the barrel of his blaster rifle rising to face Jolson. "What kind of backdown is this, Bob? He promised me this kill."

Gradually Jolson walked closer. "Take it up with Alberto," he said. "He's in a terrific hurry to see us."

Hockering slumped his shoulders. "I told you we ought to have a written contract with Alberto. Then when he promises you you can kill somebody he can't call it off."

"Alberto says you can come back and catch Jolson later," said Jolson. He lifted his head to look at one of the half-hidden sound-effects speakers. When Hockering's glance followed, Jolson stretched out his right arm and caught the rifle. He wrenched it away, bounded forward and slammed the weapon like a bar against Hockering's throat.

"Bob," gasped Hockering, his arms frogging up toward his neck.

Jolson hit him hard again with the weapon and drove a knee into the man's temple as he sank. Jolson jumped free of the toppling Hockering, reached for some thick decorative vines. Borrowing a hunting knife from the unconscious man, Jolson sliced several lengths of vine and trussed Hockering up, gagging him with his jungle suit scarf.

Yellow puffs of flowers fell profusely from the green bushes Jolson hid Hockering behind. Walking back to the lodge, the petals dropped away from his clothes. Near Rover, Jolson changed again. He grew larger and wider. Reaching the side of the caged lion he was a fair replica of the fallen Hockering.

"Bob, come out here," Jolson yelled. "Jolson's let the lion loose."

A tube chair clanked against a wall inside and then Rover opened the hand-carved lodge door. By this time Jolson was at the threshold, flat-backed to the left. "The lion's right there," said the puzzled Rover. His hand started to point. Jolson gave him a chop below the ear and Rover danced unevenly down the lodge steps.

Jolson thrust the tip of the rifle close to Rover's head as the manager regained his balance on the tall harsh grass. "Okay," said Jolson.

"Jolson, huh? That's a terrific facsimile of Nat." He twisted in his jumpsuit, scowled at the falling rain. "Let's go inside, or at least let me turn off the rain."

"Two things," said Jolson evenly. "How to get Jennifer back from Alberto safely, and some background on Group A and what you do."

"What kind of guy would I be if I betrayed a trust?"

Jolson said, "Tell me or I'll toss you in with the lion, Bob."

"Lion's a prop, he's a tame old fellow," said Rover. "All standing around in the rain is going to do is make me angry."

"Turn around," said Jolson, "hold onto the bars." With his free hand he got the truth kit out from under his singlet. By elongating his fingers slightly he was able to give Rover an injection of truth fluid, plus the necessary shot to counter whatever anti-truth drug might be in his system.

Rover sagged against the silver cage. The lion watched with curious eyes, poked out a curved paw and worried Rover's hair. "Stop playing around," Jolson told the lion and pulled Rover out of range. "Now, what's Group A?"

"I work on a strictly commission basis," said Rover, when Jolson had him propped against the lodge steps. "We're just a way station here in the spire. Because of the hospital facilities, and other things, we can keep people out of sight for a few days. When a snatch is made of some War Bureau person he's often slipped in here, in a case of food or supplies." Rover smiled a blurred smile. "We sock the old boy in a hospital room and nobody is wiser. A marvelous dodge, Jolson. After the celebrity is here for a while, long enough for things to quiet down, he's moved on into the Fringe district. You ever been there? Don't miss it. A really swell tourist attraction, though dangerous."

"Who takes the War Bureau men from you?"

"We turn them over to a kid named Son Brewster, Jr.," said Rover, his eyes fluttering toward closing. "He's a young lad, lives in the Fringe. Sings poetry. I don't know what he does with the WB people. My money comes from passing them along and not wondering about ultimate destinations. Though, I'd guess Son Brewster, Jr., has a way of getting them out of the city entirely, out into the cemeteries someplace. My guess, Jolson."

"Who's running Group A?" He caught the leaning Rover.

"Don't know that. Whoever he is, he's got a swell cover-up system. I get paid by Son Brewster, Jr., but I'm pretty darn certain he's not the leader. These days kids aren't above trying to run things, though."

Jolson said, "Now I want Jennifer."

"Oh, you haven't got a chance," said Rover, drifting backwards. "Alberto has her right in with him. Up on Floor Forty and there's no way to rescue her. You'd have to take out twenty guards, good men and true, armed. Not to mention all the extra underworld figures who dropped over for the wake."

"You can get up there."

"Yeah, because I know the password of the day."

"Which is?"

"Hurdy-gurdy," said the barely awake Rover.

"What?"

"Hurdy-gurdy," said Rover. "We used to use numbers for passwords but they're too hard to remember. Hurdy-gurdy is a terrific word and will get you through until six in the morning tomorrow. Tell it to the slot on Forty."

With some hunting ropes he found in a lodge cabinet, Jolson tied the groggy Rover, gagged him, and left him wrapped in a white animal skin before the simulated fireplace. Rover was developing a pink rash on his arms and face. Sometimes you got side effects with too many truth drugs injected at once.

Jolson made himself resemble Rover again, put on the manager's discarded formal dress.

The lion watched him sadly, roaring playfully until Jolson was in the elevator and climbing.

THIRTEEN

THE shaggy pink man gripped Jolson around the shoulders. "I can't believe he's dead, Bob," he said.

The double bedroom was dim, packed with dark-suited gangsters on folding chairs. The dead man, Socks Rubion, was on a table in the room's center, ringed by six tall gold candles in black stands. Heavy incense was piping in through the air-conditioning system. "It is hard to believe," replied Jolson. The man hugging him was Mayor Kriegspiel.

"Yesterday I was talking to him on the phone," said the former acrobat, "and today I'm at his wake. 'Hello, Socks,' I said to him. 'Hello, Dub,' he said in return. He was even wearing the exact same suit he's got on now. I saw him on the screen as clear as I see him on that slab. It's hard to believe."

"It is," said Jolson. Obviously Jennifer wasn't being held in this room.

"One of these days you'll see me flat on my back like that," continued Kriegspiel. "In fact, this morning when I tried a double backflip I got all woozy."

"That's nothing more than centrifugal force at work, Dub." Jolson ducked out of the mayor's hold. "Buck up."

"Someday I'll try a somersault and never live to finish it, Bob." The mayor wiped his pink face with a throwaway handkerchief.

Jolson paralleled a row of propped wreaths, reaching finally a partly open doorway. A man with puffy shoulders was leaning next to it. "Hello, Bob," he said. "Poor Socks, huh?"

"Well," said Jolson, "it happens to everybody."

"I think he looks very natural, considering."

Jolson agreed. "Alberto in?"

The man frowned. "What else would he be?"

"I'd like to talk to him, about that girl we caught."

"Hey, Nat was going to coldcock the guy from the Chameleon Corps or something," said the man. "Did he do it yet?"

"Nat did a swell job," said Jolson. "Really terrific."

His Rover appearance got him through the next room, a single bedroom with four quiet men armed with handguns lounging in it. After that came a long narrow office. "Here to talk to Alberto again," he told the medium-sized curly blond guard at the dictadesk.

The man blushed, and hung up the talkmike. "Somebody always pops in whenever I'm practicing my impressions. I can do Dan Bockman great now, plus Piet Goodwagon and Hobart MacQuarrie. I specialize in all those electric singers and comics. Nothing in drag because I consider that form of humor unhealthy. Listen a minute, Bob. 'Hello, everybody!' Pretty good vocal impression of Bill Nolan, isn't it?"

"Terrific," said Jolson. "Can I go on in and see Alberto?"

"Some voices," said the curly man as he reached for a bank of toggles on the aluminum ottoman next to him, "are all up here in the nose. Some are down in the throat. Like Bryan Joseph, I watch his show every morning. The real problem is a voice which is a blend. Take Terry Wollter, a voice like his is a real challenge. I'm working toward him." His fingers ticked off toggles. "The girl passed out a while ago. She's sort of attractive, though too slim for my taste."

Jolson clenched the fist away from the curly blond man and went through the portal the switches had opened. "Keep practicing," he said.

The door closed him in Alberto's room. The gray metal room was chill, smelling dimly of many cigars smoked. Jennifer was slumped sideways in a restraining chair, her blonde wig fallen on the bright floor and her real hair hanging over her very pale and perspiring face. Her eyes were closed and there was a row of bruises and puncture marks on her lower left arm.

Jolson saw she was breathing. Since he was Rover he did not touch her. With his hand resting on the back of Jennifer's chair, he said, "Alberto?"

There was no one else in the room. One wall was taken up by an old-fashioned computer. Small lights blinked and spools of memory tape jerked. Jewels, bright red and flashing green, were set into the computer's polished surface and many of the dials and knobs were gold-plated.

A two-inch slot in the computer's middle snapped open and cigar smoke spiraled out. "Hi, Bobby," said the machine's speaker grid.

"Hello, Alberto," Jolson said finally. "Nat did a terrific job on that spy Jolson. I came on back to see if you'd dug me any more information out of this girl."

"Nothing, Bobby," said the computer. "Dumb bimbo keeps passing out. Dames, they're either deadly or a drag."

Jolson said, "Why don't I take her out and dump her

someplace, Alberto? We're not going to learn anything else."

Alberto exhaled more smoke. "I never figured why they programmed me to smoke cigars. All it does is foul up all kinds of delicate mechanisms I got inside. You think Socks looks natural?"

"To me," said Jolson. He found the release switch on the back of the restraining chair and thumbed it. The chair relaxed its hold and Jennifer began to fall. Jolson caught her, lifted her free of the chair. Catching her he'd almost knocked over a tube-legged portable table.

"I guess there ain't no reason you shouldn't haul the dame out. Your problem anyhow, Bobby. I only questioned her as a friendly gesture and to keep my hand in. You sit here all day, smoke cigars, play a few games of chance, you get restless. Working somebody over, perks a guy up. You know, they got some of them new computers you can carry one around in your mitt it's so compact. Maybe they get rid of me someday, Bobby."

"You'll always be on top, Alberto." Jolson noticed a door that might lead to a private elevator. "I can take her down in your elevator there."

"Sure thing," said the computer. "Try to not bump her off unless you really have to, Bobby. Kill for business only, and as little of that as possible. I don't even know why they took the trouble to rub out Socks. Who was he hurting? Nobody."

Jolson lifted Jennifer into his arms—she was light—and started toward the elevator. "Hard to say, Alberto."

A pattern of minute green lights flashed on suddenly across the computer front. "Hold it," said Alberto. "Uh-huh, uh-huh. I see, yeah." Angry smoke rumbled out of the machine. "I just got a message from the guy who cleans the animal pens on Thirty-five and guess what that guy tells me?"

"The lion's got the pip?"

"No, this guy informs me he finds two guys wrapped up like presents down there. One of them is Nat Hockering and the other is no less than Robert Leslie Rover. Which you don't have to be a computer even to get the point of. No sir, the point is that you, buddy, ain't Bobby at all but really that lousy Chameleon Corps guy. Boy, I keep asking my lawyers when is an outraged citizenry going to wake up and crack down on guys like you. Yeah, the Chameleon Corps and the Political Espionage Office are infringing all over the rights of the individual. Coming in here, poking around, sticking on Bobby's face as though it was yours. It's invasion of privacy."

"At least," said Jolson.

"Well, Mr. Chameleon Corps, I'm going to wipe you out. You and the broad both. Take you for a one-way ride, fit you for a concrete kimono, feed you a dose of lead. Or some equally terrible thing I got filed in my tapes. You bum."

Resting Jennifer in a nearleather chair, Jolson said, "Who put you together?"

"Talking ain't going to save your bacon, schmuck."

"I'm curious," said Jolson.

"A group of the best hoodlums on Esperanza did it," said Alberto, letting out more smoke. "They formed a kind of syndicate. See, I was shipped out here originally to keep track of cemetery plots, locations and vacancies and like that. These criminal guys hijacked me and made a deal with Bobby to set me up in the funspire here. They fed into me all they knew about the crime business. All the rackets, dodges and details. Then they persuaded every crook and gangster in the whole Barnum System to make a tape of their own individual wisdom and experience for me to store. Another smart thing we do is subscribe to a lot of government printing and tape houses, under assumed names on all planets. So anytime there's one of those crime commission studies or reports, or maybe a symposium on organized crime by a lot of them smart double-dome types, we acquire all that dope, too. I got more crooked input put in me than any other computer you can name."

"You say you're good at games, too?"

"Sure I am," said Alberto. "I sit here all day, I work out them things in my head. I make up systems, how to beat the odds. I got a great boccie-ball system figured out. I ever get to Murdstone, the only place they play it in this system, and I can clean up. Mainly, I'm here to plan capers, and give legal and technical advice to the boys. I can do that real fast-like."

"About the games," said Jolson. "Do you play against real people?"

"Darn right," said Alberto. "Right on that little table you and the dame almost smashed being clumsy."

"And you win sometimes?"

"Huh? I always win. Nobody beats Alberto."

Jolson stroked Jennifer's back with his palm. "Sure, that figures," he said. "They let you win, to keep you content."

"Computers always win," said Alberto. "I don't need no boat-race kind of setup."

"You say you're good, and you're a gambler at heart."

Jolson grinned at the machine. "Take a chance, play against me."

Alberto chuckled smoke. "I already know I can beat you. No contest."

"I'm challenging you, Alberto. We play a game. If I win you let me and the girl go. You win and you go ahead with your original plan."

"A mug's wager," said Alberto. "I can't help winning. So I might as well rub you both out right away and save lots of time."

"You tell me you can win," said Jolson. "Prove it, bet on it."

"Okay, you dumb punk," said the computer. "Since you're challenging me, I get to pick out what we play at."

"Cards would suit me. You good at that?"

"I'm good at everything," said Alberto. "I ain't in the mood for cards. I'll tell you what. We'll play something the guys around here don't like. It's a board game. Yeah, we'll play that and I'll beat your pants off."

"Board game?" asked Jolson. He left Jennifer and moved a chair to the opponent's side of the tube-legged table. "Come on now."

"You want to gamble with me, buster, you do it my way," announced the computer. "I want we should play Monopoly."

"A kid's game?"

"Yeah, that's what these mugs say all the time. Bobby has a table for Monopoly down on the casino floor, though, and it's very popular. You sit down and we'll see if this is a kid game or not, wise guy."

A narrow panel slid away on Alberto's front and two metal alloy hands emerged on delicate metal arms. "I built these myself, special for games. I got another set for playing cards and musical instruments."

From a larger slot jumped a long yellow game box. Jolson caught it, tilted off its lid. "Want me to be banker?"

"No, I'm always banker." One of the metal hands scissored the box away from Jolson and thumped it down at the edge of the table. "And I always use the little vinyl puppy dog for my counter."

"I'll take the top hat," said Jolson, watching Alberto flap open the board for the game.

When the Chance cards and the Community Chest cards were down Alberto dealt out the multicolored play money. He then rubbed his hands rapidly together—they made an amplified insect sound—and said, "Remember you asked for this, buddy boy. I'm going to whip you so bad your phoney head'll spin around."

"First put down the Chance card you palmed," said Jolson.

The entrance door was pounded on and the curly blond guard shouted, "Alberto, we found out that guy in there is a fake. Why have you got your master lock on? I can't get my toggles working even. You okay?"

"Relax, De Fuccio," said Alberto. "I got the situation completely under control. Go away, let me have some fun." Alberto sorted his Monopoly money into piles. "What were you mouthing off about, punk?"

Jolson said, "When you laid the Chance cards out you palmed one. I thought this was a gentlemen's game."

The computer rotated his right hand. There was a small orange card hidden there. "Machine oil, must have made it stick."

"Collect two hundred dollars," Jolson read from the

card. He picked it off the computer's hand, put it in the pile, shuffled. "I don't think much of a guy who cheats at Monopoly."

"Shut up and play. I'll give you the first toss of the dice, eagle eyes."

Jolson rolled a five, landed on a railroad and bought it. "Your turn."

Alberto rattled the dice in his polished hand, shook them out. The dice showed a pair of fives and that put his dog counter in the jail square. "All your bickering made me shake bad."

Jennifer moaned, a bad-dream-in-a-deep-sleep sort of moan. On his next turn Jolson bought a power company.

"I guess you spies get a lot," said Alberto, blowing smoke on the dice in his cupped hands. "The way you're always working with these girl agents." Alberto got a two and landed on Jolson's power company. He paid the fee for landing there. "Some of these girl agents they aren't exactly zoftig but even a wisp of a girl agent is okay now and then if you want to change your luck. Sure, you get cooped up with a slender girl spy you can get just as horny as if it was a nice hefty broad. I figure."

"All this talk help your game?"

"No," said Alberto. "I'll keep quiet, big mouth, and beat you silly anyhow."

The game continued in silence, with Jolson playing carefully and gradually building up his control of the board. Alberto hummed to himself, muttered, whistled and smoked. He played a more reckless game, plunging and speculating.

There were two watch faces decorating the wide surface of the computer. The nearest had numerals set with precious stones. When an hour of the game had gone by, De Fuccio, the blond guard, drummed on the door again. "Is he hurting you, Alberto?"

"Go away," said Alberto. "I got him cornered."

"Cornered?" said Jolson. He rapped his finger tips on his pile of currency. "What you ought to do, Alberto, is quit now and have a good mechanic in for a tune-up."

Alberto's fist slammed the table and little hotels and houses danced on the streets of the game board. "They'll need a mechanic to put you together, loudmouth. I'm going to buy this lot I just now came down on and then I'm going to buy a bunch of houses and then turn them into big hotels and when you land on there, smart guy, you'll be all washed up."

"What are you going to use for dough?"

Alberto bunched up the last of his play money. "You sit back and act calm. The heck with that. Passion is what it takes to win at Monopoly. Don't worry about my cash."

Jolson turned to look at Jennifer. The girl was still in a deep sleep. "You put up one hotel too many," he said when he returned his attention to the game.

"Boy, what a stickler you are," said Alberto. He made a ring of his thumb and forefinger, flicked the extra red hotel off the board. It pinged into the far wall. "I got you now anyhow. I watch and wait and spring the trap."

Jolson kept avoiding the trap and when the computer's counter came to rest on Jolson's water company Alberto couldn't pay the sixty-dollar fee. He mortgaged some of his property and the game went on.

Another half hour and Alberto had nothing left to liquidate. When he drew a hundred-dollar fine he wasn't able to pay. "Damn," said the computer. "Wiped out. Boy oh boy, how could that happen?" He rubbed his hands together slowly. "Look, you can't leave it like this. You got to give me a chance to make a comeback. What say to another game, pal?"

"Nope," said Jolson. "You made the deal. Are you going to keep your word?"

"But I always win," shouted Alberto. His metal hands grabbed the edges of the game board and he upturned it. Cards and counters and houses and hotels rained on the table top, spilling off onto the floor. The computer made a grunting noise. "Well, you're right. I can't have you think I'm some kind of crumb. All right, you and the dame can go. Blow right quick and don't never come back to my place. Or I might forget I'm programmed to be a gentleman. A bargain is a bargain, a deal is a deal. Use my private-entrance elevator and get out."

In ten minutes Jolson was outside, taking Jennifer away from the funspire in a landcruiser cab. The girl was not so pale now and as they traveled the bright night streets she began to come awake.

FOURTEEN

THE flying vegetable glinted red in the morning sunlight and the smooth blond man on the tailgate of the hovering cruiser ducked, and smiled horizontally. "That's perfectly okay," he said in his deep, level voice. "It's healthy to express your aggressions in physical ways. The Social Welfare Patrol understands that." An Esperanza-grown green tomato hit him over the left breast and he smiled again. "In some of the lower socioeconomic enclaves on some planets such actions as are being exhibited here today would bring severe criticism. Such is not the case on Esperanza and here in the Fringe, boys and girls. Still another good example of the kind of civic enlightenment I'm trying to tell you about."

"You're talking through your conk," yelled a thin youth in a handed-down purple jumpsuit. He hand-putted a melon at the fluttering cruiser. Seeds spattered across the bright SWP seal.

Jolson, at the edge of the crowd of two dozen Fringe kids, put his hands in the pocket slits of his tight-fitting, vaguely military, bright orange suit. The warm morning breeze flicked at his dark braids. He was lean now, about twenty years old in appearance.

"You flats," said a youth in a long narrow blue suit, "don't comprehend the basic problem, Stoops." He shook his head and his lemon-colored ringlets bounced. "You've got a ponce's view of life, because you're in the pay of a corrupt local administration. Here, Stoops, let me quote part of a recent piece by Sol S. Mahones."

"Kubert," replied the blond SWP man, "you're not going to stand there and shout whole chunks of that nonsense at me." He bobbed away from a pale pink banana. "Rather, let me simply confront you with the facts. Where else, Kubert, but in a fair and square city setup could you be running as a free-lance candidate for mayor?"

"Up your gigg," said a girl wearing a striped awning.

"Thirty-two per cent of the food slated for your SWP outlets in the Fringe has been sidetracked into resort smorgasbords," charged Kubert.

Stoops seated himself on the tail gate, crossed his legs and let his white-booted feet swing casually. "I'd say the figure was more like eighteen per cent, Kubert. You've made the mistake of adding normal spoilage statistics to it." He clapped his hands. "Now then, I came here to dedicate this new Social Welfare Patrol Free Cafeteria." He gestured over the heads of the group at the faded lower cottage in a six-level cottage apartment building.

The wind gusted and a loose shutter fell free of one of the simulated stained-glass windows. "The place isn't worth a magg," called a blond-braided young man. "Sol S. Mahones counted seventeen diseased rats in the kitchen."

"Like your mayoralty candidate," said Stoops, "Mahones exaggerates. SWP policy has always insisted on a rat count below five in any of our facilities. In fact, I didn't see a single diseased rat in there at all during my recent tour of inspection. If you'll now allow me to step down and cut the official ribbon, we can open this splendid new free eating place at once. Yet another fine example of the kind of thinking Mayor Kriegspiel is capable of."

One white boot lowered over the tail-gate edge. Kubert, the free-lance candidate, jumped loose of the crowd and grabbed at the boot. "The Props are tired of SWP gob." He twisted Stoops off balance and down into the dusty gutter.

"A real politician wouldn't fear honest debate," said Stoops as Kubert threw himself on him.

"Flimp him," said the awning girl.

A girl next to Jolson cried, "The Munis are coming."

That would be the Municipal Police Corps. Jolson eased away from the fighting and began walking. Some spoiled fruit he couldn't identify sailed over his head and smashed the cottage window with FREE CAFETERIA hand-lettered on it. High-pitched electronic wailing was growing louder at his back. Jolson trotted his way through the scattering Fringe crowd, dodged around a corner and ran a half a block.

This whole area had been built, a full generation before, as middle-priced residential. The architects and contractors favored the then popular stacked ranch-house style, where from five to ten one-level houses are piled on top of each other to form a building. The district had shifted down-scale during the past half-dozen years. It was now called the Fringe and given over mostly to youth and poverty.

Somewhere in the Fringe Son Brewster, Jr., was at work for Group A. Jolson, a tall lanky twenty and calling himself Will Roxbury, had to find him. His new identity was a made-up one and didn't have to be as carefully back-grounded as the earlier ones. He had new ID materials, some cash and chargecards and an hour's conversation with the recovered Jennifer on the customs of the Fringe. This was his first hour here.

Jolson slowed, cut across a rutted cobblestone street and angled around another corner. A narrow, beam-fronted cottage said to him, "Common as light is love."

Spotting the speaker grid under the gilded door knocker, Jolson answered, "I'm not looking for a gooseberry slum," and hoped Jennifer had given him the Fringe vernacular right.

From fairly near a Muni siren sounded. The cottage's small window sign read "SOUVENIRS OF THE FRINGE." Jolson checked behind him, went in.

He was in the family room of the cottage. It functioned as a shop. Curved and buckled shelves hung from all the walls, and dangling on wires from the beamed roof were posters, calendars and signs. "Catch many tourists?" Jolson said.

Directly below a "Love is enough, though the world be a-waning. Join the Props!" poster was a small slender young girl of about eighteen. She wore a roseyellow shift and her hair was long, a pale auburn. She had thin arms, long legs. "You new in the Fringe?"

Jolson said, "Yeah, just came in, third-class, from Murdstone. Right now I'm avoiding the Munis."

"I'm Kath Hofstadter."

"Will Roxbury."

"I manage this shop off and on for the Props."

"That's," said Jolson, hearing no further sirens, "this guy Kubert's Amoure Propre Society, isn't it?"

"Right," said the girl. She sat on a fiber packing case.

"Lanny Kubert got the name from some old Solar System planet jargon. It means self-love."

"Son Brewster, Jr.," said Jolson. "He's in the Props, too, I heard."

"Sure," said Kath, her fingers tapping her knee. "Son's in most Fringe things. He's the one who gets these, you know, posters and all. There's a, you know, shoestring zombie plant on Peregrine someplace that makes them. Son arranges the printing and smuggling in. All the slogans, though, I write."

"Love looks not with the eyes, but with the mind," Jolson read off the top poster in a stack beside the girl. "Well, sounds better than the stuff they put on balloons over in the city."

Kath steepled her fingers under her chin. "How'd you get to look around outside this district? The Munis don't like us to wander over there. Walk around there much and it's, you know, spending some time locked up or worse."

"I saw a documentary about those funspires and their environs," said Jolson. "Back home on Murdstone."

"Anyway," said Kath, "when I said write, I meant only, you know, copy the lines out of books and off reference spools. 'Great Quotes from Many Universes' and storage tapes like that."

"How long have you been in the Fringe?"

"About a year this time," the slender girl told him. "My folks are, you know, on Barnum. My father manufactures war toys. Hofstadter Playthings, with Toys from Fifty Wars and One Hundred Police Actions. You maybe have heard of him, then."

"Yes, even on Murdstone," said Jolson. "I had one of

those Rural Pacification Kits when I was about seven."

"It must have been an antique one," said the girl, her brow wrinkling, "because some committee made Dad drop that item over twenty years ago. I'm pretty good at the history, you know, of the company. I heard it considerably as a growing person."

The door of the shop slammed open. Jolson pivoted around, his hand moving for the small blaster pistol now next to the truth kit under his arm. "Huh," he said.

The pale dark-haired man who came into the poster shop was Sol S. Mahones, whom Jolson had last seen under a table in the best part of Esperanza City. "Hi, Kath," said Mahones. He held out a hand to Jolson. "I don't know you, but I'm on the side of the Props and the Fringe ethic."

"I'm Will Roxbury," said Jolson.

"Sol S. Mahones," said the reporter. "You find me roaming the Fringe again today, Kath. My favorite pastime."

"I thought you specialized in corruption," said Jolson.

Mahones leaned against a shelf of souvenir love dolls. "There's corruption aplenty here, Bill."

"Will," corrected Kath.

"Will," said Mahones. He scratched at one of his sharp elbows. "Not only the corruption lures me here, as Kath can testify. How old would you say I am, Will?"

"Forty."

"Thirty-four," said Mahones. "That's okay you overestimated. I know that to you young people my kind, my rigid overage kind, I know we all look like walking relics. Even though I am thirty-four, Will, I understand you young people. I get inspired, emotionally inflated, breathing in the heady air of dedicated youth. Isn't that true, Kath?"

"He likes to breathe in the heady air of dedicated youth," said the girl.

"Did either of you ever hear of the Reisberson Movement?" asked Mahones.

"No," said Kath, echoed by Jolson.

"A political uprising on Tarragon about a hundred years ago," the reporter explained. "I was about to observe that Lanny Kubert and the Props are the most exciting youth movement since the Reisberson Uprising." He made wing motions with both hands. "Have you had a chance to read all these signs, Will? 'Love is swift of foot,' 'Love is like linen,' 'Love rules the court, the camp, the grove,' 'Love laughs at locksmiths.' My generation, Will, Kath, my generation doesn't understand the messages written here."

"I'm not too sure of the Love is like linen one myself," said Kath. "Son told me they wanted some with lots of *l*'s. Zombies like to letter *l*'s."

"Son," picked up Mahones. "Son is the greatest poet since William Oliver Hickey. No, the greatest since Jerrold Sunlite Ross. My generation denies it; they would. They even attack Son. Did you see the recent smear of Son Brewster, Jr., on the Barnum Indy Net, Will?"

"Missed it."

"It was a typical old-guard attack by so-called liberal reporter Floyd Janeway, a relic of the past. A man in his fifties. Now there, Will, is a man who really looks forty and not thirty-four. He looks fifty. He is fifty. That great daredevil correspondent Janeway made rude fun of Son."

"Janeway, he's the one with Barnum News Synd and the Solar Nine-Plan News?" said Jolson.

"The same, daring Floyd Janeway, with his affected eye patch." Mahones snorted. "Did you know Janeway was here on Esperanza? Not digging out corruption—he's too busy for that, above it. No, he's on some mysterious mission. The kind of junk all the slick, old-folks' media like to feature."

The door opened suddenly again. In rushed the blond Social Welfare Patrol man, Stoops. "There you are, Kath."

"First Lieutenant Hugh Stoops," said Mahones. "The handmaiden of the old fogies."

"You got your rat data wrong in your report on the new cafeteria," said Lieutenant Stoops. "I'm sorry, Kath dear, but you're going to have to come down to headquarters with me. The Simulations Bureau has developed some interesting theories about you."

The girl stood, swayed. She held out a hand toward Jolson and he moved quickly to steady her. "Will, I don't want to go there."

"What is it?" Jolson said to Stoops.

"None of your affair," said Lieutenant Stoops, "is what it is. Simulations has a pickup order out on Kath. She can't be working here when there's a PO out on her." He fingered a gray punchcard out of a gold-buttoned pocket on his tunic. "Here's an exact replica of it."

"You're not going to take any action like that against this kid," said Mahones. "I'll expose you on four hundred and thirty-two outlets across the Barnum System, if you do."

"As soon as the Munis round up a few more rioters," said the SWP man, "they'll be coming here, Kath. They're empowered to use force on you. I'll be forced to ask for their help if you don't come voluntarily now, as much as I favor reason over a raw show of force."

"What does Simulations do?" Jolson asked the trembling girl.

"They'll put me to sleep, forever."

"No one has indicated such a course," said Stoops. "The part played by the Simulations Bureau has been greatly overblown, especially by people like Mahones here."

"I have plenty of information to refute you with," said the reporter.

"I guess," Jolson said quietly to Kath, "we can't let them take you."

"I don't want to," she said. "He promised me at my last SWP interview that there was no chance of it. That's why I stayed in the open."

Stoops had his fists on his hips, facing Mahones. This put the back of his head and the slightly fat back of his neck toward Jolson. Jolson briefly tightened his hold on the girl, then let her go. He lowered his head, inhaled and then brought his clasped hands down hard on the SWP man's neck. Twice, and then again.

Stoops groaned and his knees slammed into the floor. Jolson chopped again and Stoops expelled breath and slumped limply down and out.

"I could have reasoned him around," said Mahones.

"There a back way out?" Jolson asked the girl, taking hold of her.

"Yes, and we'd better use it," Kath said. "Sol, watch the stock and try to reason with Hugh Stoops and the Munis. Thanks."

The girl pulled Jolson with her and they ran together

through a storeroom and a smoky kitchen and into a
bricked alley. No sirens came yet.

Legs up, knees close to her chin, Kath sat on the rose-
yellow bed. "The Simulations Bureau, you know, they have
computers. It's a branch of the Social Welfare Patrol. All
the data on a person, me for instance, who SWP takes an
interest in goes into their machines. And they make a pro-
jected profile of what your life is likely to be, five, ten
years into the future. A person with a future looking too
black, somebody who's going to be forever a drain, they
just remove from the Fringe."

"You're sure they really kill people?"

"Lieutenant Stoops denies it," said the girl. "He says
all that happens after a Simulations Bureau negative report is an order to transport you to some other planet. All
they care about is your not being an expense to Esperanza.
But stories keep coming out about how some people, especially those who have argued with SWP, really don't turn
up where they're supposed to be sent. You get put to
sleep and shipped to one of the potter's fields right here
on Esperanza." She hugged herself. "I don't want that to
happen, Will."

"No, it won't," Jolson said. "Is it possible to hide out
from Stoops for long, stay here in the Fringe?"

She shook her head. "I doubt it. If Stoops can't find me
in a couple days he'll put the Munis on it full-time and
they can bring electronic trackers in. A few days I could
hide, not much more."

"Well, how about getting off Esperanza?"

Kath smiled sadly. "I could go home another time," she
said. "Until I get foot-loose again. There's a remote pos-

sibility, you know, when you reach twenty-two or so you settle into something, somehow maybe."

"It would be a temporary solution, like most," said Jolson. "Do you want to try going home?"

Kath hesitated. "Instead of Simulations, yes."

"I'll get you clear. You'll need a passport, a good fake one, and some cash."

"Yes," said the girl. "How can you swing something like that, Will?"

"I have a knack," he said. The room they were in was on the third floor of a stack of cottages ten blocks away from the souvenir shop. It had originally been the appliance room before being turned into half of an apartment. Pipes and outlets stuck out of the walls and an old musical dishwasher was sunk in one corner. "Are you sure Stoops won't think of looking for you here?"

"Nobody knows I know Turkus," said Kath. "This is his place, when he's not roaming the cemeteries, running with the grave raiders. No, I'm pretty safe here, at least for a day or two. Until Lieutenant Stoops gets really mad and, you know, calls in the Munis."

"Who's Turkus? Can you trust him, in case he comes home?"

"He's half android."

"Huh?"

"Turkus had an accident when he was fifteen, his people were on welfare, back home on Peregrine. They couldn't afford repairs from the human parts centers. They had to use old surplus android parts. He's a nice boy."

"Stay here then," Jolson told her. "I'll get back to you by nightfall. Now, Kath. I have to see Son Brewster, Jr."

She started to rise. "Don't ask him for help, Will. He can't be counted on."

"This is something else. I have to find him. Where does he usually hang out?"

The girl said, "The Seven Types of Ambiguity a lot, in Bascom Alley. Or the Ultimate Chockhouse."

"I know that one," said Jolson. "Fine, I'll see you again after dark tonight."

Kath left the bed and caught his hand, she shot up and kissed him. "You're not a bad person, Will." She stepped back, her head bent down. "Or whoever you are."

Jolson said nothing.

FIFTEEN

THE two magenta player pianos collided on the diamond-shaped dance area of the Ultimate Chockhouse and the foot pedal of the bigger piano ejected and hit the fat woman who sold spray-on hallucinations and knocked her into her barrow. Three other pianos kept racing around the basement room, each playing a different tune. Jolson ordered another ale and watched the girl who was suspended from the ceiling by cadmium plush ropes pump her silver bicycle.

"Bless you, addlecove," said a turn-collared man who was keeping himself from falling over with the help of the empty chair at Jolson's green saran-covered table. "I haven't laid gagers on you before, son."

"That's right, autumn bawler, I'm new to the Fringe," answered Jolson.

The man was small and big-chested, with a bobbing chin. "Would you mind a man of the cloth sitting and wagging the velvet with you?"

"Go ahead," said Jolson.

"They call me Rev Cockspur," said the reverend. He crumbled into the empty seat, stroked a fleck of scrambled egg off his worn elbow. "That's a nice benjamin you're sporting."

"I gooseberried it."

Rev Cockspur smiled, massaging his smooth wide neck. "We all have our weaknesses, my boy."

"What is it you do exactly?"

"I'll order a bingo first, if you don't mind."

"Long as it's not on my tab."

The reverend shook his hands. "I have an arrangement with the management. Free bingo." He signaled a chrome-plated waitress. When his drink arrived the reverend added, "I don't suppose you'd care to be converted."

"Right. Is that what you do?"

"Originally," said Rev Cockspur. He tossed down his greenish liquor. "I came out to Esperanza three years ago, sent by my religious association to convert young people. I selected the Fringe to begin, to start bringing them under the wing." He waved for another drink, pinched his nose. "Wish I had a little balsam, enough to let me get my daddles on a journey."

"You take drugs, too?"

The reverend frowned into his fresh drink. "Initially I realized I wouldn't have a chance of reaching the young people of the Fringe unless I learned their ways, otherwise they'd write me off as just another joskin. First I picked up on their way of talking, after which I acquired their drinking habits. It brought me much closer to them. To press even nearer I started joining the kids on drug experiences. So, now I've reached a position where I can really communicate with them and I'm an alcoholic, a drug addict, a prescription-drug fiend and I'm living with two albino nymphomaniacs in a third-floor ghetto down the street."

Jolson tasted his brown ale, drank. "A setback," he said.

"Well, it's a good experience," said Rev Cockspur. His head snapped back and he laughed. "There's Son himself, one of the landmarks."

At the beaded doorway was a slender boy, his white hair

braided, with scarlet ribbons tied at its ends. He had on a silver-flecked jumpsuit and fawn boots. Strapped to his back was a mandolin, swinging in his left hand an illuminated amplifier.

"Son Brewster, Jr.?" Jolson asked the reverend.

"None other."

"Muck," said Son Brewster, Jr. He angrily swung the mandolin into a front playing position and dropped his amplifier on the steps.

"He's going to do one of his protest compositions," the reverend explained in a lowered voice.

The wheeling pianos quickly parked and Son touched a pick to the glistening strings of his mandolin. "I was sittin' across the street gettin' my hair clipped," he sang. "An' the barber dropped a hot towel down my damn neck. What kind of universe have you money-grubbin' bastards made for us when a thing like-a that can happen?"

"Delightful," coughed Rev Cockspur.

"Doesn't rhyme much," said Jolson.

The reverend bent toward him. "That's an unenlightened viewpoint, indicating you don't have the usual youth's understanding of the Fringe music and the ethic behind it, my son."

Son was strolling to their table, saying as he came, "Hello, Rev. Need any ned?"

"I could use some, Son. The old nock's twitching for a journey."

"Hold out your fams an I'll slip you a few rags, Rev." Son flicked a folding of bills out of a trouser slit and gave them to Rev Cockspur. "Who's the sam?"

"Friend of mine." The reverend counted the money with a ridged thumbnail.

Jolson said, "My name is Will Roxbury. You?"

"Son Brewster, Jr.," said the young man. He sucked his cheeks, slitted his eyes. "You're new in the Fringe."

"Yeah, in from Murdstone."

"Let's get to know each other. Want to play a game of zenits with me?" asked Brewster.

Shrugging, Jolson said, "Sure. How much do you want to bet on each game? Cans or dews?"

"Ten at least, dews." Brewster carefully disengaged himself from his mandolin. "Watch this for me, Rev." To the dozen young people in the shadowy room he announced, "The new sam and I are a-goin' to play some zenits."

Up above the girl climbed off her bike. A redheaded boy said, "Snitchel him, Son."

Zenits were rectangular cards with pictures of the major Esperanza cemeteries on them. They were pitched against the wall from a distance of ten feet and the player whose card landed nearest the wall won the toss. In half an hour Jolson was eighty dollars to the good. "Enough?" he asked Son.

Son tugged at one of his white braids, sucked his tongue. He took his set of cards back from Jolson and returned to his mandolin. Sitting down near Rev Cockspur, he began to sing. "When I went walkin' into the Free Barnum Information Library this mornin' they tol' me my book was three days overdue, hey. What kind of sod-kickin' universe is it when things like that can-a happen to a man." He straight-armed his mandolin to Rev Cockspur and came over to Jolson, who had an elbow resting on a silent piano. "Doing anything tonight, Will?"

"No, why?"

"Know where The Sprawling Eclectic is?"

"Yeah."

"Why not meet me there after dinnertime. We'll have some bingo and sawney, maybe play us another few games and like-a that. Okay?"

Jolson turned away. "Sure, we'll see." He headed for the doorway.

In the cobbled alley he collided with a gray old woman selling used funeral wreaths. "If you happen to know anyone named Axminster who's just died I can let you have a real bargain," the woman said.

"Make-up doesn't work any better than a wig," Jolson said.

"Damn," said Jennifer.

With a hand on the girl agent's slender back Jolson hastened her away from the Chockhouse. "You're supposed to be resting up. How do you feel?"

"You've got old-fashioned ideas about medicine. The best thing to do after being drugged is to walk around in the fresh air," said Jennifer. "Are you finding out anything?"

"I just met Son Brewster, Jr. Going to meet him again later on tonight. Is that why you're wandering around in this awful disguise, to get progress reports?"

"I wasn't even sure for a second it was you, Ben. All these kids here look alike," said the girl PEO agent. "No, I have some news, and maybe it'll tie in with what you dig up. Nat Hockering has left the city. We were still letting him roam, with a tail. He shook that early today and seems to have slipped out of Esperanza City completely."

A tourist bus was loading across the street. Before boarding, a woman with dyed hair stopped to film Jolson.

He rubbed his cheek and said to Jennifer, "No idea where Hockering was headed?"

"No, only that he was last seen on the edge of the city, beyond here. We assume he's out in the cemeteries someplace. That could mean Group A has some kind of headquarters or hideout there."

"Yeah," said Jolson, "that's what Robert Leslie Rover thought."

"Rover isn't around either," said Jennifer. "The man we had watching him says Alberto may have done something to Rover."

"He could be going where Hockering went," said Jolson. "What about Tripp from Nepenthe, and Ambassador Kimbrough?"

"Tripp tried to get off-planet and PEO had him detained on a circumlocution kind of charge."

"A PEO specialty. Kimbrough?"

Jennifer said, "The Barnum government doesn't want him charged with anything, to avoid any kind of public hearing. He's being allowed to quietly resign and retire to one of his motels."

Jolson selected a great petaled flower from the tray Jennifer was using as part of her disguise. "I was going to look up one of your PEO contact men. Probably you can speed something up for me, Jennifer. There's a young girl who's in trouble with your Social Welfare Patrol, among others. I want to get her off Esperanza, tonight if possible. I'll need a fake passport, some cash and a passage to Barnum."

"What's the girl's name. Do you have photos, fingerprints, retinal patterns?"

"She's Kath Hofstadter, daughter of the toy company

people. I didn't have time to get photos and the rest. You can get them out of somebody's files, can't you?"

Jennifer smiled sideways at him. "Yes, no problem. This is another side of Ben Jolson. I'll find out where her dad and mother live, pick a spaceport on Barnum near there."

"Good. When can I get the stuff?"

"Say seven tonight. There's a little brainwave shop on Maxwell Lane. Use the numbers, the proprietor will give you the packet. Need anything else?"

"Nothing, thanks," said Jolson.

"How did you know it was me so quickly?"

"You have nice cheekbones. You can't hide them with white powder. Besides, you're still wearing the same perfume. Details." He grinned, touched her arm and walked away.

Another tourist called to him to pose for her but Jolson didn't stop.

SIXTEEN

JOLSON listened in the twilight room. He called gently, "Kath?" The old appliance room was empty, the girl was gone.

Loud, across the hall someone suddenly began singing. "Death don't have no mercy in this land. No, death don't have no mercy in this land." The voice was deep, burred. Accompanied by the sharp sound of a metal-stringed guitar.

Jolson looked out past the unlockable door of the apartment. Part of Kath's thin face showed at the door opposite. "Over here, Will. Turkus is back and we were trying, you know, to cheer up old Mr. Grout."

"You sure you picked the right material?" The Grout apartment had been made from the entertainment room and adjoining bath.

"That was Turkus but he can't help it," said the girl after Jolson had entered.

Turkus was six feet tall, seated on a viewing chair, a huge metal guitar on his knee. His strumming arm was pocked chrome from the elbow down, as was what showed of his right leg. "Kath told me you saved her from the hamlets," said Turkus. A shoulder twitched and he began playing again. "It's a mean old world to try to live in, a mean old world to try to live in." He stopped, smiled slowly. "Sorry. Some of my parts used to belong to a circuit-riding android singer back home. He must have gone in for a lot of old country hymns. Fairly frequently, I start doing them. I've made some additions and emendations as I grew up, but I can't seem to shake his repertoire."

"When you're on the dung heap you consider anybody good company," said Grout. He was an indefinite-looking man, probably overweight. He had fluffy colorless hair and rimless glasses. "Over the hill at fifty-two. You youngsters, you don't understand. Still it's better having people around who don't understand than no people at all." He swung a hand up and rested it on the entertainment room's control panel. "I can't offer you any hospitality, young fellow, since my money is next to nothing." He nudged a toggle and the far wall filled with naked ballet dancers out of focus. "All I can ever get is some awful educational shows from a vegetarian satellite I keep demanding a repair man of the Social Welfare Patrol but they say educational television will possibly re-educate me back into the job market. Who'd hire a fifty-two-year-old naked ballet dancer?"

"Kath," Jolson said, close to her, "I have everything you'll need. We ought to leave, fairly soon."

She put her fingers to her mouth, bit a knuckle. "Should I really, you know, leave Esperanza completely?"

"Yes."

Grout poked a switch and the wall blanked momentarily, then returned with an orange-tinted snowstorm. "This is the Royal Meteorological Society weather report. More snow, followed by winds of gale intensity. All lobster cruisers are grounded."

"I'm not even sure what planet the weather reports come from," said Grout, "this room is so botched up. At least I'd like to know where it's snowing. Or even what a lobster is exactly. When you're on the wrong side of fifty-two little bits and pieces of information are what you cherish."

"Just a closer walk with thee," sang Turkus, then apologized.

Kath rested her palms on her backside. She nodded to herself. "Yes, Will, we'll go then."

Grout said, "When you're a codger nobody wants you. Once a week I go down to the Vocational Lottery. I never get lucky, never. Once they offered me a paper route on Murdstone but you had to have your own motorcycle. They even offered me the job of chimney sweep in this very building. Impossible for someone of my obviously sturdy build, I told them so. In my better days I was a free-lance pallbearer. I migrated here, figuring you couldn't help but get pallbearer work, and plenty, on Esperanza. I didn't reckon on the unions. The few funerals I did get hired for, the rotten union picketed them and sent sprays of wildflowers spelling out 'scab.' I finally couldn't get anyone to work along with me. Standard for pallbearers is an even half dozen. A one-man free-lance pallbearer service is doomed from the start."

"We have to be going, Mr. Grout," said Kath. "Turkus, thank you. We'll see each other sometime again, you know."

"No doubt," said Turkus, saluting her with his real hand.

"Do you have to rush off?" Grout asked. "The night hours are coming on."

"Yes, we have to go," Jolson told him.

"I remember I have a pot of maté hidden away under

the whirlpool bath. We'll see about heating it up for a farewell toast," said Grout.

Jolson guided Kath to the exit. "No."

The door opened from the outside and Lieutenant Stoops smiled sadly in. "Kath, Kath," he said. "Were it not for helpful older people, such as Mr. Grout, it would take SWP days to track down strays like you."

"You called the Munis?" Turkus asked Grout, rising.

"No, I called the Social Welfare Patrol. They pay a fee for information leading to the location of lost people. When you're out of the mainstream of life you take money as it comes."

"Scab," said Turkus, swinging the big metal guitar at the older man.

Avoiding the instrument, Grout said, "But you and I can still sit around and occupy each other's time, Turkus."

"I have two Munis streetside," Stoops pointed out. "Any violence of any kind will cause me to whistle them up. Any more trouble from you, Turkus, and I'll see that your name sinks to the bottom of the waiting list for spare parts."

"And me?" said Jolson.

"You're Will Roxbury. I haven't been able to find out much about you as yet. Eventually, though." He reached for Kath.

Jolson jumped back and kicked out. His heavy boot toe spiked the Social Welfare Patrol man in the kneecap. Lieutenant Stoops doubled, one hand forking for his holstered stun rod.

Jolson vised Stoops' neck with his hands and spun. Stoops galloped a few steps, left the floor and cartwheeled into the far wall. The wall flickered and another weather report came on.

Grout shouted, "Help, Munis. Youthful violence."

Turkus swung the guitar again and caught Grout just below the sternum. He stopped, sang, "One of these nights about twelve o'clock, this old world's going to reel and rock."

Grout was on his knees, using an arm to propel himself to the doorway. "Munis, Munis! Youth aflame in 403B!"

Jolson had followed Stoops. The SWP man rattled his head to clear it and Jolson brought up a short punch to his chin. Lieutenant Stoops jerked, bit on air and sank, his uniform buttons and piping making nail-scratch sounds on the wall.

"Munis, help!" shouted Grout in the hall.

Turkus caught him from behind and tumbled him back inside. He stunned him with a slap to the temple. "Will, I have a rope between this roof and the next one, for quick escapes. If you can get across you can go down through the next building and come out on the street around the corner. Take Kath, I'll stall the Munis if they come."

"They'll get you then," said Jolson.

Turkus grinned. "You don't know Esperanza law. Anybody who's part andy can't be tried. I'll get on Stoops' sam list but not much more. Now get going."

Jolson pulled Kath out of the apartment. Around a corner of the hallway an elevator door opened. "Where's that chimney Grout talked about?" Jolson asked.

"All the C apartments have them," Kath said.

Jolson ran with her to the door of 403C and pushed her inside, following. No one was home in this converted living room and kitchen. Jolson went to the hearth and stuck his head inside the fireplace pit. After a moment he saw a new star flickering in the darkening night sky. "You should be able to shinny up, Kath." He yanked the fake passport, space ticket, cash and chargecard packet out of his tunic. "You're logged off-planet at eleven tonight. Esperanza City Spaceport Number Two."

"You coming with me now?"

"Trying to," said Jolson, pressing the things into her hands. "In case I lose you. Now, upwards."

"Right." She entered the deep fireplace and Jolson's cupped hands boosted her up until she got a handhold on the rough nearbrick of the chimney. "This'll be awfully narrow for you."

"Climb," ordered Jolson.

As Kath's feet lifted out of sight the apartment was entered by a lone Muni. "Hold it."

Jolson could hear another Muni in Grout's apartment. "She's hiding off in there," Jolson said, pointing to the kitchen alcove. "I hardly know the harp, she's nothing. You crushers don't want me."

The Municipal Police Corps man's face was busy with bright freckles. He had a laser pistol on Jolson. "Show me where she is. Quick now."

Jolson backtracked into the kitchen and put his fingers on the blue enameled door of the walk-in pantry. "Down in this closet, hunkered behind a sack of kelp meal, officer. She's small and you probably would have missed her if I hadn't helped out."

"Stand clear."

Jolson stopped next to the cooking and thawing counter and used an elbow on the control toggles. A portable thawing unit pinged softly and began to glow red. "Right in there."

The Muni tilted back, gingerly spun the opening knob of the pantry door. Into the cool darkness he said, "I am obliged to inform you that you have the right to an attorney, miss. And also I must caution you that if you do not surrender swiftly I will be forced to take whatever steps I feel necessary to cause you to surrender. I am a fully qualified Municipal Police Corpsman and soon as you step out here where there's some light I'll be more than happy to properly identify myself."

Jolson threw the hotplate at the Muni's gun hand. The hand sizzled an instant and the man cried out. Jolson caught his laser pistol before it hit the floor and used its hard barrel to prod the Muni into the open pantry. He tapped him across the back of the skull with the handle and the man dropped inside unconscious.

Jolson sprinted to the chimney, slipped the gun away and jumped up. The square tube of the chimney was too narrow for him and he wedged. Jolson stretched himself, thinned and snaked fast up to the roof. He climbed out onto the gritty roof and was Will Roxbury again. "Kath?"

"I was waiting," the girl said. She stepped from behind the chimney and took his hand. "Turkus' rope is back over here."

"Fine, we'll get you to the spaceport."

"You think maybe, you know, the Munis will spot me."

"We'll get you a simple disguise for street wear," said Jolson. He'd been told, by Jennifer's contact man, that no one would be allowed to make trouble for Kath once she got on the spaceport grounds.

"Can you disguise me well enough to fool people?"

"Yes," said Jolson.

SEVENTEEN

THE ceiling was fretted with plastic plumbing and circuitry. The thin strips of wall lighting were blotched with puffs of orange fungus and the small basement rooms were dim. Son Brewster, Jr., all in gold, skirted around a tangle of rusted toy cruisers and stopped next to an askew stack of dusty space luggage. "Why the Friday face, Will?" he asked. He spun once and his electric mandolin danced on his back.

"This isn't much of a flash panny so far," Jolson said.

Son smiled and dodged through a low buckled doorway. He pointed upward, said, "Topside people can't accept things as they are. The Sprawling Eclectic is a club where things are left alone. It's a warren of storage rooms, under a stack of apartments. You're going to like it, Will. Wait."

Stepping around a sprawling pool of muddy water, Jolson said, "Not too crowded tonight."

"Some rooms are, some aren't."

On a pile of old overcoats against the wall of this cubicle a plump bristly young man was sitting quietly with his hand on his chin. "Love is like linen," he remarked.

"Yeah, I've been wondering about that," said Jolson. "What does it mean exactly?"

The bristly young man shrugged one shoulder. "I read it on a poster."

One more room along Brewster nearly tripped over an open sample case ringed with rubberoid wine bottles. He kicked at one with a golden boot. "Earth vintage, California. That stuff doesn't travel well."

Flat on his back in front of a bin of firewood and used fuel cells was a compact blond man. Jolson recognized him as Peter Terraloma Gooden, the field man with the Derelict Research Foundation, whom he'd met at the spaceport on arrival.

Jolson bent beside him, nudged him with a thumb. "Who's this cove?" he asked Son.

"Named Gooden, a market research man," said Brewster. "He's gathering data."

"Whee," murmured Gooden, rolling hazily from side to side.

Son guided Jolson on, through other shadowy cluttered rooms. Sitting in one, his feet up on a ruined clothespress, was Rev Cockspur. He was clutching his left hand with his right, releasing it, watching it quiver, clutching it again. "Bless," he said.

Opposite him, on an oil-leaking dishwasher, Lanny Kubert, the free-lance Prop candidate for mayor, was working on a hand recording machine, using a small bright screwdriver. "The incidence of shoddy manufacturing practices is on the upswing. Bitched-up dictating machines are thirteen per cent more frequent this year than last, Rev. There, I got her going again."

Cockspur inflated his big chest, released his fluttering hand. "Play back what we have so far, Lanny."

Kubert depressed the playback button. "Field Report Number 237," the dictating machine said in Cockspur's voice. "Regarding conversions among residents of the Fringe. Dear Executive Bishop . . ." The voice dimmed and faded.

Rev Cockspur caught his nose. "This is always the most difficult part of the report, the part we're getting to now. I should keep better records. A little bingo, Lanny."

Kubert put the recorder aside and jumped from the washer. "That Earth wine Gooden jettisoned okay with you, Rev?"

Cockspur said, "The Santa Cruz forty-seven has an excellent bouquet, for an Earth wine. Join us, Son and Will?"

"We're heading for the Appliances," said Son. "Bingo spoils an Appliance journey."

"A little gelter," said Rev Cockspur, "just a touch of ocher and I'd journey myself. Once I get my spiritual business out of the way I may see what I can do about a small journey. Bless you all, coves."

"Appliances?" asked Jolson.

"Tonight doesn't feel like a moll night to me," Son told him. "Let's leave the owls alone and try a journey for ourselves."

"Look," said Jolson as they left the room. "You said I'd get a jomer here, meet some real shakester harps. You may be in the mood for hallucinations, I'm more inclined toward women."

Son grinned and tossed his hair. "You haven't seen the Appliances. I got five of them, from a hackum I know in the city proper. He runs a funspire and gave us a good deal on a batch of used hallucination machines. These are the flawless ones, Will. You just put some realmoney in, you take your journey and you're back in a half hour with no side effects, no fuzzy reconnects. We'll do it now. Later maybe we'll find a couple of owls I know. They used to be convent girls on Murdstone, tall willowy harps. The kind you like."

"Who said I liked skinny girls?"

"A hunch," said Son.

From a damp room to their left a voice said, "Hey, Son, I have to consult you."

This room was filled almost entirely with wired bundles of photocopy newspapers. A spike-haired nearcat was hopping from pile to pile, tracking an unseen rat. On a straight-back chair sat Sol S. Mahones with an antique typewriter in his lap.

"Hi, Sol," said Son. "Working on an assignment?"

"Yes, a piece for a Barnum print weekly. They still won't take verbal copy, say it dehumanizes the reporting." To Jolson Mahones said, "This boy is like a torch on a dark night, the greatest poet since D. B. Yellowstone. Son, I'm sure you have a protest song about the Barnum Child Conscription Bill. I'd like to quote it."

Son took a fold of flesh above his waist between his thumb and forefinger and thought. "What's the Child Conscription Bill?"

Mahones looked up. "The bill to allow the central Barnum government to induct kids from ten and on into public works projects."

"So," said Brewster. He reached over his shoulder and unslung the mandolin. He flipped the instrument's cord to Jolson. "Plug it."

When Jolson bent the nearcat hopped on his back and began purring behind his right ear. Jolson hunched the animal off on a scattering of headlines and found an outlet for the mandolin. "Set."

"Huh," sang Son Brewster, Jr., "I was a-walkin' to school the other day, a-thinkin' how much an education can help you in this universe, an' some damn authority dragged me off to take part in a corrupt civic project. What the heck for?" He yanked the cord free of its plug, shouldered his mandolin.

"Beautiful, Son," said Mahones, single-fingering the typewriter keys. "Was that 'corrupt civic project' you said?"

"Something like that," said Brewster. "Let's move on, Will. Appliances are only a couple of turnings away."

The Appliance rooms were in a row, off a gravel-floored corridor. "I'm still," said Jolson, "in favor of just meeting some girls and drinking bingo."

Son Brewster, Jr., opened a silvered door and pushed Jolson through. The narrow room held a pinstriped cot and a silver-finished waist-high hallucination machine. Jabbing a metal dollar into the slot, Brewster shoved Jolson hard toward the cot. "Hallucinate first, then drink." He backed out quickly.

The machine purred and a faint floral wreath smell began to grow around Jolson. He flat-handed himself off the cot and went to the door. It wasn't locked and he got it open easily.

"No hallucinations tonight," he said in the corridor.

He noticed the gravel was now made up of smooth white egg-shaped stones, here and there a stone was a soft rose-yellow in color. His bootsteps made the stones rub together and give off a dry insect hum.

He'd find Son Brewster, Jr., and hit him with the truth kit right now. If Son was alone in one of these Appliance cribs it would be a good time to question him. Jolson opened the nearest door. "Excuse me," he said.

Mayor Kriegspiel was behind the door, turning lazy somersaults on top of a hand-carved desk while his naked girl secretary watched. The wallpaper applauded after each completed turn and the mayor, who was wearing only a pair of pinstriped shorts, would pause to bow.

"Let me return to a point I made earlier," said a voice at Jolson's back. He turned.

"I must have missed you before," Jolson said to old Dr. Anthony H. Davis-Stockbridge of the Chameleon Corps Academy. "It's good to run into you, sir. Particularly since I had the idea you'd passed away."

The gravel eggs were waist high now and Jolson's old teacher sat down on them in a relaxed tweedy position. He leaned back against air. "Perhaps, Mr. Jolson," he said, "we should begin with a review of what we have learned so far. My respects, by the way, to your father."

"He passed away," said Jolson, "two years ago."

"I'm sorry to hear that. I didn't know."

"Usually," said Jolson, resting on a boulder that had grown up next to him, "I don't talk about it much. Or other personnel matters, like Jennifer Hark and so on. What was it you started to ask me, sir?"

All the stones were growing larger and they forced Jolson and Dr. Anthony H. Davis-Stockbridge up toward the ceiling. The doctor used his tired, freckled hands to part the pipes and painted-on wires. "You were always one of my favorite pupils, Mr. Jolson, though I don't imagine I was ever able to convey that to you."

"No," said Jolson. "I didn't even know you knew how to take ceilings apart."

"Control the alpha rays and you can do anything," said the old man, spreading flooring and vinyl panels, so they could continue their ascent. "To return to the issues. How have you been progressing on this particular jaunt?"

Jolson said, "Here, sir, I'll show you." He turned himself into Leonard F. Gabney. "This is the first one I did on this mission."

Davis-Stockbridge stroked his chin, where a beard was starting to grow. "Very good, Mr. Jolson. An excellent impersonation. A trifle cruel perhaps, with youth's lack of understanding of age, but a good performance nonetheless. I'll see that you get a gold circle."

"I didn't know you graded that way."

"We had to drop the poetry," said Davis-Stockbridge, "but please to continue."

"My next one was this," Jolson explained and turned into playboy Gilbert Gillespie, following him with Robert Leslie Rover and then Nat Hockering.

"Excellent, Mr. Jolson," said Davis-Stockbridge. The pipes and energy conduits were twining themselves with the old doctor, some of them growing wispy gray hair. "I'm afraid there's a great deal of Academy business to be attended to now."

"I haven't even showed you Will Roxbury yet," said Jolson. He rose from the pinstriped cot and pointed five fingers at the room's door.

The hallucination machine clicked and a speaker grid below a flashing red bubble said, "Repeat, repeat. Deposit of another dollar is urgently required. Otherwise your session must now be terminated. This is your last and final warning."

Jolson lowered his head for a second, made a sighing exhalation. He walked carefully to the bright surfaced machine and knelt. He caught his reflection in the metal and he was still Will Roxbury. He nodded, stood. He reached for the door handle, then stopped. He had the wrong hand. It was an old man's hand, veined and worn, age-spotted. And the left hand matched it. After a moment Jolson was able to change them and when he stepped into the corridor he was completely Roxbury.

"Quite an experience," said Son Brewster, Jr. He was resting against an abandoned forced-air bike. "A real spiritual experience, isn't it, a journey? Rev Cockspur agrees. Enjoy yours?"

"Some," said Jolson. "You?"

"Always do," said Son. "Follow me a few rooms further. I want you to witness a group of my friends perform. After that we'll check out the owl situation."

Jolson went with him, crossing the gravel with care.

EIGHTEEN

A bigger room, with piped water gurgling beneath the just-swept nearstone floor. Personal mementos of past tenants were heaped against the walls. A dimensional triptych of a jungle vacation wavered and dropped onto the makeshift crate-lid platform in the center of the room On the platform four white-haired boys in scarlet jumpsuits and ivory boots were setting up instruments, tuning, testing connections and amplifiers. A bass fiddle, three guitars, a forced-air sitar, a turbosax and a computerized viola.

"Will," said Son Brewster, Jr., "meet Dal, Hank, Butch and Gramps, the Sprawling Eclectic Jug Band. They're friends of mine, do mostly my material."

"Son is a better lyricist than Jordon and Gordon," said Hank. "Or any of those other old-time song-writer bastards."

"You forgot to pack the jug again," said a very tall black-haired girl who entered from a dark doorway. She was dressed to match the Jug Band, carrying a squat aluminumized carafe.

"Mimi," said Son. "She's the publicist for the group. Mimi, this is Will Roxbury."

"You told me about him," said the girl. She was taller than Jolson and smelled of religious incense.

"We'll play something until a crowd gathers," said Butch on the bandstand. "One of Son's."

The Jug Band began playing and a diploma sliced out of its frame and drifted off a pile of mementos. Gramps sang, "Two weeks ago Tuesday I went into a cafeteria and was a-orderin' hash. An' they told me they were all out of hash. What kind of god-awful universe is it when they can tell a lovin'-hearted young man things like-a that?"

"What's your home planet, Will?" asked Mimi.

"Murdstone," answered Jolson.

"A coincidence," said Son. "Mimi was just there for a vacation."

"You have some lovely dances on your planet, Will," said the tall girl. She held out a hand. "Join me."

Jolson's short briefing hadn't covered this and he and Mimi had an odd time on the smooth nearstone floor. Son extracted a dusty tambourine from among the piles and he sat in with the Sprawling Eclectic Jug Band, watching Jolson try to dance. After two fast protest numbers Mimi stopped and said, "I'll take a rest and go round up some bingo."

"And a few more harps," said Butch.

The moment the girl stepped into darkness the group put aside their instruments and leaped from the low platform. They circled Jolson and Son Brewster, Jr., said, "Yep, you're a fake for sure, Will. Robert Leslie Rover told me there was a Chameleon Corps man a-prowlin' around and I've been testing strangers. First place, you play zenits with the old rules nobody has used for a decade. Maybe you played that way at the Academy."

"You're still on some kind of journey, Son. I don't understand you."

"I got a peephole a-lookin' in on your journey room, sam. An' I had a little extra something mixed in with the hallucination blend. I saw you going through your shape changes when you were flat on your ass on the cot."

"Okay," said Jolson. He shifted position and his foot clicked against a brass ring set in the floor.

"I just used the dance business for frosting."

"He sure isn't attuned," said Gramps. "Nobody dances like that on Murdstone any more."

"You don't even talk quite right," said Son. "You look like one of us almost, but you haven't got the velvet down. And you don't really move young."

Jolson elbowed through the group, jumped and swung up on the music platform.

"Snitchel him," shouted Son.

Each member of the Jug Band fetched out a battery-operated carving knife.

"Flimp him good," ordered Son.

Jolson grabbed up the bass fiddle, swung it out hard by the neck as the first member of the quartet came springing.

"He's pulling a mingus," warned Gramps.

Dal, the one who took the bass full in the stomach, snapped his head in biting jerks, crashed back into stacked souvenir menus.

Hank slashed straight up with his buzzing knife. Jolson hit the floor, planted himself and swung up with clasped hands. Hank growled and doubled over. Gramps and Butch came at Jolson together, knives augering air.

Son Brewster, Jr., had his fingers hooked on the brass ring set in the floor. He strained and a trap door grated open, the pipes sounded nearer. "Get him and we'll dump him down in the sewers."

Jolson stretched his left arm and wound it round Butch's neck. He unwound with a harsh pull and Butch spun into

Gramps and over-ended him. While the pair was floored, stumbling upward, Jolson gave each a chop across the neck. They slumped and he hurdled and dealt a similar chop to Hank, who was almost upright again. Dal's wind had returned and he ran at Jolson with his whirring knife held like a lance.

"Dirty snaffer," said Dal.

Jolson bent, side-stepped and tripped the running Dal. The last conscious member of the Jug Band flopped down, skimmed over the floor and whacked his head against the raised trap-door lid.

"Now then," said Jolson and walked toward Son.

Son shook a raised hand. "I don't want any violence from you, Jolson. I won't enter into any roughhouse."

Jolson took the brass ring away from him and pulled the trap door fully open. Water throbbed and burbled in the dampness and dark. Jolson caught Son by the back of the collar and yanked him off balance. He swung him over the pit, head down. "Tell me about Group A."

"Don't drop me in there," said Son. He strained until his chin was resting against his shoulder. "You take it easy, Jolson. They've got your girl."

"What?"

"The harp with the funny cheekbones. Jennifer. We spotted her talking to you and tagged her. She's PEO and Group A has her now."

"Where is she?" Jolson lowered Son Brewster, Jr., until his braids were touching the nearest water-beaded pipe.

"Come on, I don't like this down here."

"Tell me."

"Jennifer Hark is on her way to the isle."

"What isle?"

"It's beyond the cemeteries, about four hundred miles from here. Where they keep the frozen bodies. The isle."

"Who's got her?"

"You watch it, sam, you're dragging my hair in the diddle."

Jolson pulled Son up, spun him and caught his tunic front. He sat him over on the platform and said, "Go on."

"I'm telling you, sam, you better watch it. They froze that bitch over an hour ago and if you make me any more trouble I'll see they keep her that way."

Jolson slowly put his hands on the boy's shoulders. After a few seconds he said, "Who took her to the island?"

"Some of Group A's agents, I told you. They hauled her in a hoodoo wagon. To get to the isle you drive straight out the main highway through the cemeteries. She'll be there before morning."

"What's your part in Group A?"

"After the snatchers get the target guy I set up the transportation. We use some of the cut-rate funeral wagons operating out of the Fringe. You can't fly over the cemeteries, you know."

"Who's on the isle, who's running Group A?"

"I don't know."

Jolson moved back. "Tell me now, Son."

Son rubbed his chin. "Well, I do know his name, I've heard that. His name is Purviance. Maxwell Purviance and he believes in something like Earth being supreme."

"What's he after, that or peace?"

"I really don't know, Jolson. I'm too involved here in the Fringe to keep up with everybody's ideology. Purviance pays pretty good. Who knows what he's thinking about?"

Jolson swung a stiff hand and tapped Son Brewster, Jr., twice at the temple. The young man passed out and fell on the viola.

Using instrument cords and souvenir pillows and shawls, Jolson got the Jug Band and Son trussed up and gagged. Three rooms beyond this one he found some half-filled storage closets. He carried the young men there one by one and left them in the narrow compartments.

In a few more minutes he was out in the streets of the Fringe. He ran for a loading stop when he saw a tourist bus marked Cemetery Express about to pull away. He sprang on just before the doors snapped shut, found a seat. The bus rolled, aimed at the cemeteries.

NINETEEN

TOMBS and monuments blinked red and yellow and green beyond the bus windows. This particular cemetery had apparently been filled at a time when equestrian monuments were popular. On each side of the wide dark roadway stretched row on row of mounted figures, their simulated marble rotating from red to yellow to green as the banks of ground-level spots went through their quick cycles.

The two-chinned woman next to Jolson was sobbing into a plyo handkerchief. Jolson said, "Going to visit a close relative?"

"No, young man," the woman said. "I don't know anybody on this whole planet, dead or alive."

"I noticed you were crying."

"I'm fond of horses. Whenever I see so many of them depicted it breaks me down."

A near-bald man in front of them turned around. "You two folks on the Econtour?"

"No," said Jolson.

"I'm on a three-weeks-on-three-planets flight plan," said the heavy woman, wiping at her puffed eyes.

"My name's Lowenkopf," the man said while the lights from outside turned his head green. "I take an Econ to Esperanza once a year when there's a slack period at the pornography shop I run on Barafunda. This year I'm doing chemists."

"Chemists?" asked Jolson, spotting a vacant seat further up and across the aisle.

"I visit only the tombs of famous chemists. Last year I did actors. Chipped a hunk off Hasselbadd's crypt. Remember Hasselbadd? Lots of folks don't, but once everyone called him 'The Man You'd Love to Give a Big Kiss.' Hasselbadd was very big on wallies in my youth."

"I always come for the flowers," said the woman. "Flowers and horses are my two ruling passions in life."

"One year I just rode the roller coasters," said the bald man, turning to face the driver's end of the bus.

"Palomino," said the woman, nudging the window.

Jolson got quietly up and took a new seat. "Excuse me," he said to the wide-shouldered, very blonde girl he was now next to. He reached under himself and handed her a roll of photocop magazines.

The big girl wrinkled her nose, smiled left-handedly. "Fanzines," she said. She patted her bare knees and laughed. "I'm actually a fanzine writer."

"Are you?" said Jolson.

"Am I what?"

"A writer for some kind of fan magazine."

She slapped her knees, wrinkled her nose. "I'm a greenhorn in the business. Otherwise I'd be faster on the uptake. I'd sense your questions and field them better. Yes, I write for a chain of cemetery fanzines, based back home on Murdstone. The Sensible Friendly Publishing Empire, maybe you've heard of them?"

Jolson said, "No."

The girl lifted her shoulders, dropped them. "I hadn't either. Originally I was just a dumb dicta-andy dispatcher and then one day I said heck and quit and wrote a novel."

"A novel?"

"Maybe they don't have them on your planet. It's like a magazine, only thicker. About growing up, love, early sorrow. It didn't sell to anybody but it was something I had to do and then I got this job with Sensible Friendly. We write up all the cemeteries on Esperanza, all the ones most popular with fans." She wrinkled her nose at the window. "Horses aren't very big this year. Things go in peaks and dips."

"People," asked Jolson, "buy your magazines to read about cemeteries?"

"Exactly," said the big blonde. "I guess I'm kind of incoherent explaining it all to you. See, this is my first fact-finding excursion out here. Up until now I was on the lobster desk, that's what we call it in the fanzine world, on the lobster desk putting field reports from Esperanza into Sensible Friendly style. We have a distinct style of our own."

"Don't read much," said Jolson. "Visual stuff, that's what I like. And noise."

"Of course," replied the blonde. "You're in the eighteen to twenty generation. I myself am in the twenty-three to twenty-five generation and there's a certain, what we call, generational gap between yourself and me."

"Ever," said Jolson, "hear of this freezing process place, an island out beyond the cemeteries?"

"Yes," said the girl, "but we've never written it up. Not too many cryonics fans in our audience, according to the polls we take. Those people on that isle, the things you hear."

"What exactly?"

The blonde said, "I don't know anything exactly. The

girl who manned the lobster before me, she was full of gossip and she told me a reporter for some fanzine went out there once a couple years ago and he never returned. She said she bet they froze him, put him on ice. She had stories like that, quite a few."

The equestrian cemetery ended and patches of thick dark forest showed on both sides of the road. Across the night highway thin glistening mist began to drift, close to the ground. "You've heard nothing else?"

"No, not about the isle. She told me Merle Murmac was gay but I don't believe that. We put out a lot of media fanzines, too, at Sensible Friendly."

A row of twice-life-size gilded statues came up on their side of the misty road. "New cemetery," said Jolson. "What's the motif on this one?"

"Well, those statues aren't monuments," explained the girl reporter, "they're awards. This is Cemetery No. Fifteen and it's always getting the Freddy. That's an affectionate term for the Frederick P. Dickerson award. Number Fifteen has won six. Which is a record. Two for aptness and originality of lawns."

"Seven-hour rest stop ahead," the bus driver announced on his speakers.

"Huh?" said Jolson.

"All the buses pull off the road at midnight," the blonde reporter said. "The turnpike is too dangerous after that. I know it's hard to believe, considering this is more or less sacred ground, but at night all sorts of difficult people prowl the roads. Ghouls, grave robbers, bandits, highwaymen and that like. There's a pretty fair coffee shop at the Eternal Sleep Motel up ahead. If you don't feel like turning right in."

"I have to keep moving. I thought this damn thing went straight through all night," said Jolson. "I caught it on the run as it was."

"No, none of them do any more. Too much trouble has been had," she said. "When we stop I'll buy you coffee, or whatever drink it is you drink on your planet of origin."

"Damn," said Jolson. He started to rise, then sat.

In a few moments the big bus roared off the highway and stopped in a red graveled lot next to the Eternal Sleep Coffee Shop.

"You can sit up all night," the blonde girl said. "See the sign."

Jolson glanced. "Yeah," he said. Below the ruby-tinted WE NEVER CLOSE were parked two landcruisers. One was labeled ESPERANZA CITY FUNERAL PAYMENT FOLLOW-UP SERVICE, the other HOBART'S HOMEGROWN MATÉ. "I'll buy you a cup of maté."

"Oh, swell," said the blonde girl. "My name is Mary Jane, which you probably didn't know since I forgot to tell you."

"Will Roxbury," he said as they went up the entrance ramp.

The place was an old-fashioned drop-seat one, with each table and its chairs sunk in an individual pit. Only two of the twenty some pits were occupied, despite the recent arrival of a nearly full bus.

Seated down in a pit, Mary Jane wrinkled her nose and poked at the service control dial panel. "I don't see any maté on here, Will."

"Right there," said Jolson. "Under ginger beer, Number Twenty-Two." He dialed two cups, stuck a chargecard in the pay slot.

"Vanity. I never wear my corrective eyecaps. I think it spoils the color of one's eyes. Do you think that?"

The cups popped up out of the service holes in the table top. "No," said Jolson.

Two pits away a peak-headed man was waving a hand recorder at a fat ringleted woman in a pinstripe black suit who was kneeling at his pit rim. "This is important to me, Mrs. Erasmus," he said. "Now stop tracking me all over the planet."

"You owe ninety-five dollars still on the probate," said Mrs. Erasmus. "Sixty-three dollars on assorted carrying charges. Your permanent care fee is so overdue that weeds are sprouting all around your poor departed uncle's crypt. All the daffodils are long since strangled."

"He's not even my uncle," said the man with the recorder, rising up in the pit. "He's actually the uncle of the man who used to live in my cottage. You keep sending your bills to the wrong man, Mrs. Erasmus. All I want to do is work on my lyrics, and the only place I can work in tranquillity is open-all-night coffee shops."

"You don't have to tell me your *modus vivendi*," said Mrs. Erasmus. "I've got enough info spools on you to choke a goat."

"Goats aren't native to this planet."

"Don't try any of that lyric stuff on me. You're no better than anyone else. I want the two hundred and forty-six dollars and then your poor Uncle Edwin can rest in peace. And I can close this file and spend the next couple of days in the steam baths here. As long as I've tracked you to a place with a splendid steam bath attached I'd like to enjoy it."

"Excuse me," Jolson said to Mary Jane. He boosted himself out of their pit and walked over to the crouching Mrs. Erasmus. Squatting beside her, Jolson asked, "Would that be your landcruiser parked outside, ma'am?"

"Yes, it would. Now don't interfere with my collection duties."

"Will you rent it to me for the two days you plan to spend here?"

She twisted, frowned at him. "I might, but this deadbeat with no respect for the deceased won't pay up."

"The guy she wants moved six years ago," said the lyric writer.

To Mrs. Erasmus, Jolson said, "I couldn't help overhearing your discussion and I hate to think of Uncle Edwin only partially paid for. I'd be pleased to settle the bill myself, provided you agree to rent me your cruiser."

Mrs. Erasmus hefted herself upright. "You're a young philanthropist. I had a feeling you might be, despite the long hair, young man. You'll have to deposit one hundred dollars in cash, sign an agreement in triplicate, leave me all of your ID packet but your vehicle-operating papers. A deal?"

The mist was thicker now as Jolson resumed traveling. He had to drive slowly, cautiously on the quiet late night highway.

He'd gone nearly thirty cold miles from the Eternal Sleep Motel when the rented cruiser began to make grating sounds. It yawed on the slick roadway. The machine suddenly stopped, its engine grinding and its treads spinning in an off-key way. Jolson clicked the engine switch, opened his compartment door.

He swung one leg out of the cruiser, and was lowering

toward the misted road when something clamped his foot and pulled. Jolson's spine end hit the running board and then the road and before he could yell in pain a blow over the ear felled him.

TWENTY

ABOVE one of the coffins a small window barred with rusty ornamental iron showed him an oval of thin gray morning. Jolson shivered awake, hunching. He was on a cold stone shelf, wrists tied behind him with what felt like thick wool scarves, ankles crossed and bound with gilded cords. In rocking his knees sideways Jolson knocked over a half-full sack of sweet-coated pet food. The checkered sack dropped the five feet to the crypt floor and spilled pellets over a bundle of faded condolence cards.

Jolson yawned automatically, took a deep needling breath. The half-dozen coffins in the dim room were on shelves similar to his. The nearest coffin was decorated with hand-carved pastoral scenes and while he was watching it a sheep lit up. Jolson swung his tied legs free of the shelf edge and managed to get himself into a sitting position. One of his boots ticked against a coffin and a pile of last years's television logs hopped off the top.

To the left of his hanging feet was a portable microfilm reader with an unfinished sandwich on its control panel. Jolson watched the day outside the oval window take on color. By now Jennifer would be at the isle. Jolson tried to force his hands apart, but the shaggy bonds held.

A large stained-glass window appeared at the top of a short flight of marble steps across the crypt and came toward him. IN LOVING MEMORY OF UNCLE VINCENT was spelled out in green glass buttons across the top of the window, which showed a panorama of nondenominational religious events.

Noticing plump fingers at the window's edges, Jolson said, "Do you represent the people who sapped me and trussed me up in this tomb?"

"Let me put this thing down someplace." The window was leaned against a dusty home electronic music console by a fat girl in a pastel-flowered tent dress. Her chestnut hair hung long and free.

"You live here?" Jolson asked her.

The girl scratched her wide bare ankle. "Yes. I hate cleaning up, so it's sort of rumpled around here. Do you think that's a bad trait in a woman, not liking to clean up?"

"I've never known anyone who lived in a crypt before," Jolson said. "So I don't have any preconceptions."

"When I roomed in the Fringe I wasn't any better," the girl said. She crossed the cluttered room and yanked at Jolson's tied feet, pulling him off the perch. Before he hit the floor she caught him under his arms and propped him against the microfilm reader. "My name is Nadia Lanzer and I'm nearly forty pounds too heavy for my height. Does that bother you?"

"What bothers me is being tied hand and foot and put on a shelf in a tomb," said Jolson. "Was it your people who pulled me out of my landcruiser and knocked me out?"

Nadia's round cheeks were red from the chill of the morning outside and she rubbed at them with one hand. "You're younger than I am, too. By a good eight years I'd guess. Do you like maturity in a woman? Maturity coupled with a weight problem."

Jolson remembered he was still in his Will Roxbury phase. "Could you untie me before we talk?"

"I don't have the authority to do that," she said, backing off slightly. "Even taking you off the shelf I could get criticized for. How do you feel about a woman who takes risks for a man?"

Jolson said, "Who does have the authority around here?"

"Trevor," said the plump girl. "I'm better at cooking than at tidying up. It's perfectly okay if I fix you breakfast. To me that's very feminine, fixing breakfast for a man."

"Trevor?"

"Trevor Macy," said Nadia. She took a packet of self-cooking oatmeal off the top of a floor coffin and held it up to Jolson. "I've been living with him for nearly two years. Oatmeal suit you?"

"I usually skip breakfast," said Jolson. "Why'd Macy grab me?"

"Call him Trevor," said Nadia. "He's one of those people you call by their first name. Some people they look like their last names and some like their first. He's a first-name person. Trevor."

"But why bring me here?"

"You were traveling through his territory," said the fat girl, "at night. Very few people do that, unless they're law. Like the Cemetery Patrol, them we always have to watch out for. When your cruiser stopped near where he was working, Trevor thought you might be a spy. If you'd looked like law they would have killed you there. You don't seem to be and Trevor brought you here, probably to ask you to join up."

"I'd rather move on."

"Don't try arguing with Trevor about that," said Nadia. "Because you don't have much choice."

"You loot cemeteries, huh?"

"Yes," said Nadia, watching him carefully. "Is that a touch of disapproval I see in your eyes?"

"No," Jolson told her. "I'm from the Fringe myself. I've got nothing against you."

Nadia smiled. "I gooseberried that stained-glass window myself. Real semiprecious stones in it."

Metal rattled outside, jingled. A tall broad man in a green cloak jumped down into the crypt. He had graying blond hair that hung to his jaw, a tangled mustache. When he thumped a plyo sack on the console the machine whirred for a second and played a snatch of computerized anthem. The sack was filled with old-fashioned vocal timepieces, silver and gold. "Lemon and I found these just before sunrise, where they bury that sect. The ones who believe in leaving their watches on. Got twenty of the damn things."

"That's marvelous, Trevor," said the girl. "Will here told me he's very eager to join up with us."

Trevor's grin used only the left half of his tanned face. "Hiding out from some trouble back in the Fringe?" he asked Jolson.

"Welfare Patrol wants me, Simulations Bureau."

"I can sympathize," said Trevor. "Find a blade, Nadia, and cut Will loose." He began prowling the crypt, prodding piled loot and scatters of paper with his booted foot. "Where are the application forms?"

Nadia clutched a battery-operated slicing knife out of her bodice and began the work of freeing Jolson. "On top of the lifetime wreaths, Trevor."

"I just looked there."

Trevor sat on a blank ivory tombstone. "I'll explain our operation to you, Will. We operate like guerrillas, living off the land, off people when we can. We shift our bases around. Sometimes we live in the tombs and crypts, other times out in the ornamental forests they have between some of the cemeteries. To start, your pay with us would average about two hundred a week."

"I was doing better than that in the Fringe," said Jolson, flexing his freed hands.

"No Welfare Patrol to worry about here," said Trevor. "Only the Cemetery Police and I have them figured out. Of course, Will, you don't have to come in with us. We can, instead, put you to sleep and stick you in a coffin. I really need another hand, which is why I have to be hard-nose."

"He does want to join," put in Nadia. She touched Jolson's knee warningly, then got the last of the gilt ropes cut away from his ankles.

"Sure," said Jolson.

"I used to be in the marketing line on Barnum," said Trevor. "Even though being a ghoul isn't quite the same thing, I try to run my present business along efficient lines. I have an application form for people who join up, I keep files."

"Suppose the Cemetery Police find your records?" asked Jolson.

Trevor grinned. "I've got them figured out, Will," he said. "Anyhow, I only have two people working for me at the moment. Files on two people you can miniaturize and hide pretty well."

Stroking his numb wrists and stomping his numb feet, Jolson said, "Okay, it won't hurt me to sign then."

"When and if Nadia finds the damn things," said Trevor. He rose up, began pacing. "Last month I lifted a coffee machine out of a nondenominational motel. Then I got to reading up on the effects of coffee. I don't know, you spend the whole night out exhuming things and you'd like to have a cup of nice hot coffee. They say, though, caffeine can eat straight through you."

"There's always oatmeal," offered Nadia.

"Not the same," said Trevor. "Oatmeal is simply not a very good stimulant."

"You ought to try maté," said Jolson.

"Stand a little to the left, Nadia, and I'll drop him," said a thin voice from outside.

At the window oval there was a sharp-edged pale face. A snub-nosed hand laser masked part of it. "I gave the order to cut him loose, Lemon," Trevor said to the window. "Relax and come inside."

"Is he making you say that, Trevor? I can beam him where he stands."

"Get in here and have some oatmeal, Lemon," called Nadia.

In a moment the short thin Lemon ran into the crypt, jabbing his laser pistol away in a belt holster. "I had a really good and glorious night of it, Nadia. I was a glowing, gold-hatted success."

"Trevor said," Nadia replied. "Sit down someplace."

"I was beautifully perceptive," said Lemon. He snapped a paisley skullcap off his straight dark hair. "Wearing my one and only lucky hat. Right to the watches. Right to the watches we went, Nadia. You can't beat Lemon Ernst when he is in a glistening, gold-hatted mood, wearing his famous lucky headgear. You trust this fellow here, Trevor?" Lemon Ernst whipped out a blaster rod and jumped near Jolson. "I can zap him here and now."

"Sit, I told you," said Nadia. "Or you won't have any breakfast, Lemon."

"He's all right," said Trevor. "His name is Will Roxbury."

"I know that," said Lemon. "I was the one who located his operating ID. Golden in mood, unfailing in instinct. Lemon homed right to it."

"It was in my back pocket," said Jolson. "You don't have to be too golden to find it."

Lemon laughed, falsetto. "I can take kidding, Will Roxbury. I don't zap a guy for joking with me. Sometimes, when I'm in a black mood, you know when you feel your head is full of spiders and black kaleidoscopes, then perhaps. Now, I'm relaxed and serene. Two thousand dollars at least we'll realize on those watches, Trevor."

"Fifteen hundred at most," said Trevor. "Do you know where the application forms are? Will is joining us and Nadia can't find the forms."

"Women," said Lemon, "aren't given to gold-hatted moments of locating things. I know. I spent a whole black year of my young life on Barnum married to a fat girl. Fat girls can't find things especially. They simply can not." He crossed the room, lifted an unstrung metal guitar. "Right here are the application forms, Trevor. So you're going to join the group, Roxbury?"

"Probably," said Jolson.

"You don't sound so enthusiastic," said Trevor. He

grabbed up the stained file folder Lemon had located. "Something wrong?"

Jolson pointed a thumb at Lemon. "He's your whole crew?"

"Lemon's very good. In a long career in marketing I learned how to evaluate people. Lemon is very good, when he relaxes."

"I'm chrome-finished, gold-hatted," said Lemon. He walked sideways in Jolson's direction. "Easy enough to take you out, Roxbury. Criticism makes me spider-filled and black. My second wife, not as fat as the first, was very critical." He made a rattling sound in his throat and threw himself at Jolson.

Jolson bobbed, rammed his fist into the charging Lemon's stomach and swung him between himself and Trevor. He chopped a hand against the smaller man's neck and frisked the laser pistol out of its holster with his other hand.

Lemon dropped unconscious onto the feed sack. "Now then," said Jolson, the weapon in his hand.

"Fast," said Trevor, still sorting through the forms in his folder. "Nadia, shoot him down if he doesn't give back the pistol quickly."

Jolson noticed the plump girl. She had a blaster rifle aimed at him. "We don't want you running away. Is that what you're thinking of?"

Jolson slowly rested the pistol on top of the coffin lid. "All I wanted to do," he said, "was show Lemon it isn't a good idea to threaten me."

"You'd better have some oatmeal now," Nadia said.

"And look this application over while you're eating," Trevor said. "I'll drag Lemon out and have a talk with him. He is a very good person to have working for you, when he relaxes. One thing, Will, I insist on accord."

When they were alone Nadia said to Jolson, "Were you going to escape?"

Jolson shrugged, not speaking.

"I wouldn't blame. I don't make a good first impression."

TWENTY-ONE

JOLSON looked from the rifle poised on Nadia's round knees to the chart Trevor was spreading on the picnic table. "A whole day lost," Jolson said to himself. "And no closer to Jennifer."

Twilight filled the formal forest and Jolson had to lean to see what the raider leader was pointing at. "Right here," Trevor was saying, his forefinger reiterating a red X. "The tomb is built like a geodesic dome and you'll see Mayor Chidsey's name on it in light strips."

Lemon Ernst rested his sharp nose on his fist. He had one nervous foot up on the picnic table bench. "The night makes me illuminated, Trevor. I glow with perception and become a human dowsing rod. There's really no need for a map, I'll find the place on instinct alone."

"Why Mayor Chidsey's tomb?" asked Jolson.

"Chidsey was mayor of a condominium on Peregrine," explained Nadia. "A condominium populated mostly by a sect that believes in burying its dead with all their appliances."

"This haul should get us a dimensional videoset, a ten-man whirlpool bath and an eight-track light hypnotizer," said Trevor. "Not to mention servoandies. Altogether we could get forty or fifty appliances, according to the publicity releases."

"They usually exaggerate those," said Nadia. "Still we

figure to pick up at least two dozen appliances. Roughly five thousand dollars' worth."

"And we have to carry the loot all the way from the middle of that cemetery down the hill there," asked Jolson, "to your van off in the woods here?"

"You stay with this outfit, Roxbury, and you better learn to carry things," Lemon told him. "When I am in one of my elated gold-hatted moods I carry appliances two at a time, moving like a grim zephyr."

"If the Chidsey funeral was only yesterday," said Jolson, "won't they have extra Cemetery Police around?"

Nadia said, "There are only two CP to any one cemetery and they don't make exceptions for somebody as low on the scale as a mayor. He wasn't a celebrity."

"Tonight," said Trevor, "this being your first run with us, we aren't trusting you with any weapons. Later on you'll go armed. Then any CP you meet you can put out of the way."

Lemon juggled his hand laser from left palm to right. "My official kill record is nine Cemetery Police taken out."

The high straight trees all around them turned black as the day ended. "Let's begin," said Trevor. He sauntered away from the table.

"The chart," said Nadia.

"Forgot," said Trevor. He returned and folded the stiff paper under his green cloak. "You travel between me and Nadia, Will, and stay in sequence."

Lemon gave one of his falsetto growls and went zigzagging silently away.

There were no birds or animals in this forest, no sound except the rustling of dry leaves in a faint night wind. The lights of the cemetery they had come to raid began to show as the group moved ahead. Soon names and sentiments could be seen flashing in the darkness. The fountain type of tomb was popular here and geysers of colored water sprouted beside them when they left the cover of the woods.

Trevor stopped next to a blue fountain and pointed to his left. "See it? The one with the gold weathercock on top."

From around a pillared vault came Lemon, hugging a dictation android in his arms. "Ten of these in the tomb," he said. "This one takes two hundred words a minute." He hopped where he stood and then ran for the raider van parked in the clearing in the forest.

The grilled doors of the dome tomb of Mayor Chidsey stood open. Hands on hips, Trevor stopped at the threshold, grinning in. "Look, Nadia. A good fifty appliances piled up here. I told you those Peregrine sect people don't puff up facts in their press releases."

Close to Jolson Nadia said, "Let Trevor take the heavier things. I'll give you a hand lifting. You're not used to grave robbing and you could strain something."

"I'll help you," said Jolson. "I have a more traditional approach to things."

"As we get to know each other we start finding out our likes and dislikes," the plump girl said.

Trevor was inside the vault, toying with the switch of a miniaturized floor waxer. The appliance came to life, ran around his boot and buffed a square yard of parquet flooring before he clicked it off.

Jolson entered. "We going to have time to haul all this before we get spotted?"

"My policy, based on considerable experience and backed by research," said Trevor, "is to snipe the most valuable things first." He smiled and gestured across the tomb. "That over there, the white thing with the bowed legs. You know what that is, Will?"

"A bathtub. So?"

"Yes, but a real antique bathtub, from the Earth planets I'd guess. Probably teleported here to the Barnum System at great expense to the common taxpayer. That's made of real porcelain, and it's got all the approved safety features. I can get two thousand dollars for that tub in the Fringe."

"Want me to carry it to the van?"

"We'll both heft it," Trevor told him, massaging his hands. "Antiques are heavy bastards."

At the tub Jolson asked, "What kind of percentage do I get?"

"Ten per cent. It's all explained in the employee brochure I gave you to read." Trevor adjusted his cloak and positioned himself in front of the ancient tub. "You carry the rear. Another benefit, and you can verify this with Nadia or Lemon, is that after you've been with the group one fiscal year your percentage rises to twelve point five. After you've been with us five years there's a profit-sharing plan, too."

Nadia waited until Trevor and Jolson were out in the night with the tub before going into the tomb. "I'll gather some of the lighter objects."

Trevor carried his end of the bathtub at a trot and Jolson had to follow his style. They wound their way through mausoleums and tombs, trying to keep out of the splash of the colored lights and fireworks displays. Trevor had just reached the lowest tree of the formal forest when a rasping wail hit the night air.

"Cemetery Patrol?" asked Jolson.

"Right, damn it," replied the graveyard guerrilla. "Let's double-time."

While they ran the highly amplified sirens multiplied down in the cemetery. "How about Nadia?" said Jolson.

"Our code is each for himself," said Trevor. "That's in the brochure."

A bullhorn began shouting. "This is your Cemetery Patrol for Cemetery Number Twenty-nine, requesting you to surrender. Now, here is our legal advisor to read you a prepared statement concerning your rights under the recent Esperanza Crime Commission suggestions regarding surrendering in cemeteries, including advice on how to obtain proper legal counsel. Can you all hear this clearly enough?"

"Damn," said Trevor. The tub had wedged between two close-standing trees. "Back up a second."

Jolson let go of the tub, which stayed wedged in midair, and reached out for Trevor's back. He caught Trevor's cloak and tugged him off balance, yanked him backwards, reeled him into the tub and pushed his head down hard against the porcelain. Trevor groaned and collapsed, his left foot grating against the gilded hot water faucet.

Jolson pulled Trevor's pistol free of his tangled cloak. Checking over his shoulder, he started moving fast through the trees. He covered some fifty yards and then came up against Lemon Ernst.

"My anger is blazing like a beacon in the ebony night," said the little guerrilla. "I am suffused with the pure fire of revenge. I saw you coldcock Trevor, Roxbury. Before I rescue him from the CP I'm going to allow myself the golden joy of taking you out for good and final." Lemon was holding a laser pistol in one white fist, a blaster in the other.

Jolson threw himself suddenly into the brush, firing the borrowed blaster pistol as he fell.

An instant after the sputtering crackle Lemon gave a short soft grunt. His right hand was smoky and limp, his sleeve fluttering with tiny flames. "Anger guides me like a lodestar," he whispered. He swung his good hand and its laser gun toward the doubled-over Jolson.

Jolson took more time and better aim on his next shot. Lemon's second weapon sizzled and flew like a dying meteor into the dark leaves. Lemon grunted, leaped at Jolson.

Standing full, Jolson swung a fist up. Lemon's head whiplashed. He flickered away and slammed against a wide trunk, sinking deflated.

". . . these statements, however, must be backed by reliable witnesses and they require adequate documentation and full notarization . . . ," came the voice of the legal advisor, still far below.

Jolson holstered his pistol in his trouser waist. He put his palms briefly at the side of his head, then began to run again.

"Wait."

Jolson narrowed his back, halted. He looked around and saw Nadia, a portable drink mixer against her plump side and the blaster rifle aimed at him. "I'm glad to see you avoided the CP," Jolson said to the girl.

"You certainly go to extremes to avoid me," she said.

"I like you, Nadia. I'm in the middle of doing something

else. I've lost enough time and now I have to move, to do what I have to do."

Nadia asked, "I can't compel you to stay?"

"With the rifle you have a fifty-fifty chance."

She lowered the weapon. "I'll try to salvage Trevor and Lemon before the Cemetery Patrol gets up here. You go ahead. I imagine it involves some other girl, some girl younger and less heavy, doesn't it?"

"There's a girl, yes," said Jolson.

Nadia reached into her tent dress, came out with a pronged key. "Use this on the motorbike, stored in the back of our van. I'll tell Trevor you forced it out of me. You can use the bike, the van I'll need for the boys."

"Thanks." He caught the thrown key.

"I'm always following my heart instead of my head," said Nadia. "No man can really admire that."

"I don't know. I do." Jolson bowed his head slightly and left, running.

TWENTY-TWO

T H E sky slowly brightened, the dawn chill faded. Jolson released the steering mechanism of the motorbike for a second and flexed his hands. If a recent road sign was correct, he was a short twenty-five miles from the isle. Electronic music blossomed at the roadside and the tomb of the Unknown Commando started its daylight rotations.

Over the next rise in the road Jolson almost rear-ended a wide silver landcruiser. He yanked the brake rod hard, swung to pass. On the observation balcony of the cruiser a lean, hollow-faced man, eye-patched, waved at him. "Like some breakfast, kid?"

Jolson recognized the rumple-haired man in the flower-print lounging robe. "Beg pardon?"

"Have breakfast with me? It's nearly ready inside. You look to me like one of those Fringe kids and I'd like to talk to you, get backgrounded."

Jolson's foot let up on the power pedal. "You wouldn't be Floyd Janeway, would you?" he called.

"I would, I would." The thin man with the eye patch chuckled and reached down for a mug. "Floyd Janeway; occupation: newsman."

"Stop your cruiser a minute, I'll join you."

Over his shoulder Janeway said, "Miss Sturges, tell Jimmy to halt. I'm inviting a young guy to breakfast."

The landcruiser halted and the reporter helped Jolson

up onto the platform. "You can hitch your bike to that rack there, what it's for." He sipped from his nearpewter mug. "I'm pleased to find you younger people have heard of me."

The bike attached, Jolson accompanied Janeway into the main salon of his cruiser. The room was an office, long and bright, furnished with a round, realwood desk. The chairs had realwood legs and there was a thick soft rug. Taking a cane-bottomed chair, Jolson said, "Janeway of Solar Nine-Plan News in the Earth System and Barnum News Synd out here. Sure, sir. You're a celebrity to my generation."

"No crap? That's great." The cruiser began to move again. "I worry. Guys like this Sol S. Mahones, they seem more in tune with youth. Half this universe and two-thirds of the Earth System, did you know, are under the age of twenty. It's a big market, youth."

"Are you," said Jolson, "doing another one of your famous firsthand reports, sir? In the vein of 'Twenty Days with the Tarragon Rebels' and 'Four Tough Weeks with the King of the Peregrine Jungle Raiders'?"

"Hey, you really do know my stuff," said Janeway while refilling his mug from a row of ale spigots above his desk. "Actually that was 'Twenty-One Days with the Tarragon Rebels,' but you had the gist. I'm on my way this very moment to do a big one. Not another 'Janeway Explains the Turmeric Harbor Fiasco,' no, more in the tradition of 'Janeway Up Close with the Murdstone Assassins.'"

"What is the story, exactly?"

Janeway agitated his head. "Too secret," he said into his ale. "I am sitting on something too secret to even talk about. Lord knows when I can break the thing."

"I figured," said Jolson, "you probably had a lead on Group A."

A willowy brunette girl in an off-white jumpsuit came into the room. She said, "Mr. Janeway doesn't know anything about that."

Janeway drank ale and nodded agreement. "She's correct, can't argue with her. No, this isn't that secret at all. Miss Sturges, this young man is joining me for breakfast."

"His name is?"

"Will Roxbury," said Jolson.

At his ale spigot Janeway asked, "How do you like her? Miss Sturges, I mean. That's what you call a heart-shaped face. You a heart-shaped-face buff?"

Jolson smiled at the girl. "Miss Sturges seems quite attractive, sir."

"Bull," said Janeway. "You don't have to be polite. She's an android. They used duraflex on her, one reason she looks more lifelike than your mass-product andy. The reason I asked is because I myself, Miss Sturges, am tired of that particular face."

"You'd prefer what?" the girl android asked.

"Is there anything you'd like, Roxbury?" Janeway finished his ale and refilled the nearpewter mug carefully. "I always have an eye opener before breakfast, so nobody has to look at me askew like you are, Roxbury."

"Askance," corrected Miss Sturges. She fingered open a wood-finished wall panel.

"Up your askance," said Janeway. He gestured with the full mug. "Well, come on, Roxbury. Pick a face."

On a shelf behind the panel rested ten girl android heads. "Your choice," said Jolson. "The blonde second from the left isn't bad."

"A cliché," said Janeway. "Your same typical gnat-brained wide-eyed far-from-innocent blonde. No. I almost sent that head back except I had it all wrapped and the damned mailing machine was set to print this little slogan 'Support Your Local Welfare Store' along with the postage where I was borrowing mailing facilities and I couldn't figure how to remove the lousy slogan so I unwrapped the head and kept it. If that's the kind of head youth wants, Roxy, I can't say I think much of the future of womanhood. Miss Sturges, put on the Venusian head and let's see how it goes."

The android pressed her finger tips twice to her throat and lifted her present head off. She set it on an empty shelf space and lifted out a faintly green head, one covered with finespun off-orange hair. She clicked the new head into place, licked her green lips and smiled. "Now may I get on with fixing breakfast?"

Janeway covered his good eye with his hand. "Lord, that's an ugly mother of a head. Phew. Take it off, take it off right away." He hinged his hand away from his eye, squinted at his ale and drank it down. "Hold up that Ganymede broad. Nope, nope. Too unsettling this time of day with all that flapping hair. Oh, crap, stick back on the one you had in the first place. Roxbury, have something to drink."

Miss Sturges, returned to her initial self, said, "May I begin the breakfast?"

"Roxy and I, can't you see, are having a pick-me-up, pick-us-up, before our breakfast," said the reporter. "'Janeway among the Mountain Rebels of Peregrine.' Did you ever read that one, Roxy? Did anybody in your entire cop-out generation read that particular celebrated piece?"

"Sure," said Jolson. "You won the Fillinger Prize for it, didn't you?"

"You bet your underage ass I did," said Janeway. "Miss Sturges, go turn on the griddlecake computer. I thought we were having breakfast. Roxbury, I can tell you among friends the best thing I have ever done is coming up."

The android left and Jolson said, "I have a feeling, sir, your new story is really going to do things for you in the youth arena. That is, from what little I can learn."

Janeway plopped onto a candy-stripe loveseat. "How about this? 'Janeway Calls on Purviance.' That's their damned title, not mine. I didn't pick it out. I don't think the average consumer of information knows Purviance from his kneecap. 'Janeway Gets the First Interview with the Leader of Group A.' That's better, that's what I'd rather call it. In the print version anyway. Crap, it took months of wangling to set this up and I still can't carry a camera inside there. And I'll tell you, Roxy, the Political Espionage Office would love to know where I am headed. What isle I am going to be on shortly. A newsman can't betray a confidence, though, or cross a picket line or step on a crack and break his mother's back. You do like griddlecakes, don't you? You'd better, Roxy Soxy."

"So you're interviewing Purviance, the leader of Group A himself? When?"

"This very day, you nosy little faggot." Janeway tossed Jolson his empty mug. "Get me another ale, Roxy Boxy. All you young guys now are faggots. Why Sol S. Mahones likes you. Right? Admit it."

Jolson drew a fresh mug of ale and handed it to the reporter. "You've never talked to Purviance before, met him?"

"Of course not."

"How do you get into his stronghold then, sir?"

"I have a password. One that only Janeway knows. I have to say 'Remember North Dakota!' Besides, Roxy Boxy, everyone, even some backwoods Group A buffoon, knows Janeway when he sees him. Even you, you silly little faggot, you knew me. Drink some ale like a man, will you."

Jolson stepped closer to the reporter. Janeway had both hands clutching the surface of the mug. That would do for fingerprints. In Janeway's voice Jolson called, "Miss Sturges, tell that damned Jimmy to stop the cruiser. I'm going to boot this young faggot off. Cancel breakfast and keep out of here yourself."

Janeway half grinned. "That's a great impersonation, Roxy." He turned his head sideways and then faced Jolson. "But why are you doing it?"

Janeway sat up and into Jolson's fist. The blow caught him on the chin and he dropped. Jolson saved the ale mug, peeled the reporter out of his lounging robe with one turn. He pushed one arm into the garment while he dragged Janeway toward the observation balcony. The cruiser had just stopped.

The robe completely on, Jolson concentrated, thinned and changed until he was a replica of Janeway. He'd match the prints later. He dragged the night-suited reporter to the platform, slumped him on the railing and then jumped to the roadway. The sun was warm now, the sky a quiet blue.

Jolson unhitched the motorbike and somersaulted Janeway onto its seat. He started the machine and, doubling on the seat behind Janeway, guided the bike toward a cemetery entranceway. All the tombs here were above ground, done in the suburban cottage style of a decade ago. Jolson stopped in front of a crypt out of sight of the parked cruiser. He jimmied off the cottage door and deposited Janeway on the hooked rug inside. From his drug kit he gave the fallen reporter a knockout shot guaranteed by PEO to last a full day.

He hefted the motorbike into the cottage tomb and parked it next to Janeway. He was crossing the tulip patch outside when he blurted, "The eye patch," and went back for it.

In the cruiser, lounging on the loveseat, Jolson shouted for Miss Sturges. "Let's get moving. When am I supposed to see Purviance anyway?"

"In two hours," said the entering Miss Sturges.

"He's probably a faggot."

"You think everyone is."

"Get me my ID packet and whatever else I'm going to take on this lousy interview."

The android passed him a packet and a realleather portfolio. "Right on top of your desk."

"Lord, with any head you're unpleasant to look at. Get out, drive or something and send Jimmy back here."

Miss Sturges said, "You're really addling that pea brain of yours. Jimmy, remember, is your cute nickname for the automatic driving mechanism on this cruiser."

One less person to worry about. "Well, you can still go away yourself."

Settled on the loveseat Jolson carefully studied the prints on the reporter's ale mug, compared them with those in Janeway's ID material. After he'd assumed the reporter's fingerprints he called Miss Sturges in and ordered her to bring him a double serving of griddlecakes.

TWENTY-THREE

T H E cruiser lurched and Jolson spilled ale on the automatic driver. "Sorry, Jimmy," he said, bending forward in the observer's seat of the cab. After they had passed the last monument of the last cemetery, a silver cannon on a stone block, the paved highway had ended. There was only gritty red dirt for road now as the landcruiser rose and dipped over the low hills.

Miss Sturges poked a new head into the cab. "We're about there. Are you at all presentable?"

"I'm Floyd Janeway and that should be enough for anyone," Jolson told her. He had on one of the reporter's tan jumpsuits, the reporter's ID papers stuffed in the breast pocket. "Get away from me now, Miss Sturges. You're looking very superfluous. I don't want you dragging along on this intervview with me. Remain here."

"You know you can't remember anything without me," said the girl android. "You didn't even remember the king of Tarragon had been assassinated, and it happened while you were interviewing him."

"With those guys you can't be sure when they're dead or alive," said Jolson. "If you want to be of real service, go freshen this ale."

The cruiser climbed a steeper hill, quivered, and glided down. Below, at the road's end was a large lake. Smooth and chill blue. In the lake's center, dotted with circling white birds, was a bright green isle. It was rich with palms, ferns, twisting vines, spilling flowers. At the top of a low incline rested a softly yellow building. A building all columns and fretwork and marbled leaves and rustic friezes.

"Some layout, huh, boss?" said the driving mechanism's voice grid.

Glaring white swans were drifting on the lake's stillness. "Park in that patch of wild anise," said Jolson.

On this side of the lake, at the water's edge, was a narrow black jetty. A wiry bearded man was sitting on it. The man, wearing a shaggy brown overcoat, stood when Jolson climbed down from the cab of the parked cruiser.

"Be sure you stay right in there, Miss Sturges," warned Jolson on leaving the cruiser.

The overcoated man kept his back to Jolson, watched him approach over his sohulder. "Got a load of popsicles for me today?"

"Look me in the eye when you speak to me, you overdressed lunk," said Jolson. He made his way unevenly through the red dust of the passway. "I'm Floyd Janeway, not some gay hoodoo wagon operator."

The bearded man turned his head entirely away, bent with a grunt and selected a flat white stone from a small pile near his slippered feet. He cast the stone out at the silent water and it bounced twice, missing a swan. "All we handle here is the thoughtful storage of frozen bodies, mister."

The black jetty creaked when Jolson stepped on it, swayed with his hollow steps. "Janeway, newsman. Tell Purviance I'm here."

The man turned, not quite in sync with his heavy coat. His worn slippers scattered the pile of throwing stones.

"Stop yourself right about there. Three long-range lasers are aimed right at your funky butt, not to mention a couple which'll fry your brains. Very slowly produce your identification papers. Should you also have any words or catch phrases you care to speak, this is an awfully good time for doing that."

Sliding out the Janeway ID packet, Jolson said, "Remember North Dakota. Okay?"

"Toss the papers, underhand and gentle," said the overcoated guard. He stretched to catch the packet and a plumed horse showed on his wrist.

"That's a fine tattoo," said Jolson.

"My entire body is totally covered with tattoos, mister. All depicting tombs and mausoleums. I had a morbid streak in my youth. It still makes a nice *memento mori*. At one time I was quite an attraction in Esperanza City. I had part of an entire floor in one of the lesser funspires and charged a fairly stiff admission."

"An interesing piece of background trivia," said Jolson. "Now get me over to Purviance."

"Patience," said the tattooed guard. "Let's see your hands." A dove fluttered down and landed on the thick overcoat's left shoulder. The guard reached up and pulled the bird's chest open. A small mike showed. After studying Jolson's finger tips, the guard said loudly, "He seems to be who he says. Send the cruiser."

While Jolson waited on the jetty the guard said, "I don't take as many showers as I once did. It depresses me to soap myself down."

"I can imagine."

From the columned building rose a scarlet cruiser. It

made a lazy arc and flew across the water. Over Jolson, it hovered about ten feet up and a rope ladder dropped down.

"Climb on up," called Nat Hockering.

The marble-walled reception room was cold. Jolson sat on a narrow visitor's chair and watched Nat Hockering. The former Nepenthe attendant was on the lip of a low desk, his thick fingers tangled with switchboard wires. "Mr. Purviance will get to you in a few more minutes, Janeway. Stop fidgeting," said Hockering. "It's his lunch hour."

"I don't mind not being invited to dine with your lousy employer, but I would like a drink. Ale."

"All you could get here is applejack anyway," said Hockering. "I haven't got any time to dig that out now. Forget it and wait." Hockering moved the switchboard mike up to his mouth with a nudge from his chin. "Look, Ed," he said into the mike, "you guys are supposed to handle storage problems in your offices. I don't care what she says, that's not possible. No, because Purviance Storage is the oldest and best firm in the business. All right, just a second, let me write that down." He flicked a handful of wires away and motioned to Jolson. "You're a writer, give me something to write with." He caught the pen Jolson flipped him. "Okay, Ed. Right, I got the name. I'll check but you tell her it has to be her uncle. She signed for him and if it didn't turn out to be her uncle when she got him thawed out we're not to blame."

Jolson walked across the room, away from Hockering. Two doors led out of the reception room, one marked STORAGE, the other marked PURVIANCE. Jolson stepped to the Purviance door and knocked.

"Tell her any warranty complaints have to be in writing,"

Hockering said. "I have to go, Ed." He unhooked himself from the switchboard and jumped off the desk. He ran at Jolson, shouting, "I told you wait, you booze fiend."

"Either a drink or an interview," said Jolson. "Janeway is not a man to sit around."

"You're awful eager," said Hockering. "You sure you're really this lush Janeway? We've been having trouble with impersonations."

"There's only one Janeway. And I'm it, you pea-brained clunk."

"I checked you once," said Hockering. "Any more I'm not so sure. Let me have another look at your ID stuff."

Jolson produced the packet. "We can call the whole interview off, you know. Tell Purviance that. I'm welcome in two other universes, both of which serve liquor."

Hockering grabbed one of Jolson's hands and looked hard at his fingers. "They match." He scowled, watching. "Details," he said all at once. He reached out and yanked away the eye patch.

Jolson said, "You lout."

Hockering swallowed, returned the eye patch. "Sorry, Mr. Janeway." He reached around Jolson and gave a special rap on the Purviance door.

"Yes, come in," said a voice on the other side.

TWENTY-FOUR

T H E rocking chair was cluttered with eagles. They were carved all over it, twisting and interlocking, black. In the chair, which was ticking regularly and slowly back and forth, sat a tight-mouthed man. He was wearing pull-over cloth pants, a loose shirt of fine checks and a wide-brimmed hat made of real straw. His fingers were square and smooth, holding a yellow-bowled pipe. Even relaxing in the chair the large man held himself tight. "Understand, I mean you no offense when I ask if I am right in assuming you're not Earth-born," he said, forcing the pipestem between his teeth.

"Come on, Purviance," said Jolson. He shifted on his over-padded chair. "I was born on Barnum. Most people know that. Floyd Janeway has certainly been profiled enough."

The small parlor was clothbound, with thick rugs on the floor, heavy drapes on the wall. Backstopping Maxwell Purviance's rocker was a half ring of many-legged tables, all covered with fringed cloths. Behind and above his head hung an embroidered cloth sign reading EARTH SUPREME. "I can always tell some person not born on Earth." Purviance's nostrils bellowed out once. "I sense such things, Mr. Janeway."

"Maybe what you smell is that dead cat under your chair," said Jolson, pointing with his foot.

"No, that's a fresh cat," said Purviance. "I use them to test my meals. I have the notion my breakfast must have been poisoned. Personal poisoning is always easier to catch than organized governmental poisoning. There are, to give you an instance, nineteen known poisons in your average urban drinking water. Ten were put there by the government to kill you should you step out of line, five are there to push you toward decadence and big government thinking and the remaining four we haven't been able to figure out yet but I feel they're just there for spite. I never drink water, it goes without saying."

Jolson asked, "What then?"

Purviance tapped his signet ring against a crockery pitcher on the nearest table. "Applejack, Mr. Janeway, an old, very old and traditional, Earth beverage. I never eat or drink universe fool, only Earth food. You notice I call you Mister with respect. Even though you give off an odor of the out planets. Here's an item for you, Mr. Janeway. In my files I have all the planets classified as to the way their residents smell."

"No smell like Earth, I bet," said Jolson. "Before you give me any more items, let me ask some questions, Purviance. Now, what exactly are your plans?"

"For before or after I take over?"

"Well," said Jolson, "tell me about the before part first."

Purviance took a blade of dry grass from a pocket on the chest of his trousers and hooked it over his lower teeth, next to the pipe. "Well sir, the universes, in my book, were meant to be ruled from Earth. All the planets, in all the systems, ruled by Earth. Due to an unfortunate so-called intelligence and cultural lag of twenty thousand years Earth was taken advantage of by other outside planets. My job is really very simple, Mr. Janeway. I am going to take back all the planets and rule them from Earth. Earth rights have to dominate again, as is only natural."

"I had the impression," said Jolson as the Group A leader rocked, "that you were perhaps some kind of pacifist, Purviance. A man aimed at cutting down wars."

"I'm interested in cutting down the wars I don't start, yes sir," said Purviance. A lock of his straight hair edged down over his brow and he reached up and patted it. "I started Group A so I could get control of all the war making. Call it A because that puts it at the head of the list, if you get me. I'll tell you something else off the record, Mr. Janeway. I've been recruiting a very large group of military advisors. Probably, in your journalism work, you've had an inkling of this."

"Yes," said Jolson. "You have these top-level military people living here with you, on your island?"

Purviance reached down and absently stroked the dead cat. "Pardon me if I say I'd like a drink of applejack. I don't have anybody to test it on for poison. I don't suppose you . . . ?"

"I could use a drink myself," said Jolson. "But, no."

"A pity," said Purviance.

"About the military experts you've been gathering?"

"Yes sir," said Purviance. "I've got them here. Got them on ice."

"Frozen?"

"See, Mr. Janeway, that's my cover. This is the biggest body storage plant you're going to find. We deal mostly with people who want to live later on, and not now. There are always plenty of them. We also have some really dead ones, whose folks want them preserved for various reasons. I inherited the whole operation from my late father, Maxwell Purviance, Sr. We've got him in a freezer, too, but he's dead and done for. Little tag on his freezer reads OUR FOUNDER."

"He give you the idea for Group A, too?"

"No sir, that's entirely my own," said Purviance in his tight voice. "Here's another little confidence for you, Mr. Janeway. I don't really like deep-freeze people, no sir. They're almost like dead people. They all give me the willies. We're still on a low budget, however, and I can live here on the isle rent-free and make a pretty good profit off the business, even with big government siphoning off unfair taxes. Still, Mr. Janeway, I have to admit that some mornings when I throw aside the counterpane and hop out to do my chores I say to myself, 'Maxwell, as far as the eye can see, it's just you and a bunch of bodies.' And it gives me the willies for sure."

Jolson stroked the chin of his Janeway face. "I'm beginning to understand you and Group A, Purviance. Can we look around your plant here while I ask further questions?"

"Some of it, sure enough," said Purviance. "The unclassified parts, yes sir. A lot of things are hush-hush." He inclined up out of the rocker. "A word to the wise, Mr. Janeway. You'll be under continual scrutiny while we take our little tour. In danger of instant disintegration should you make anything that looks like a false move."

"Why is that?"

"Well sir, the only way to protect the secret workings of Group A, and the Purviance freezing and storage process, is with taut security. Guards, lasers, peepholes. It's a common industrial technique from Earth that I've adapted to our needs," said Purviance.

"How many members do you have in Group A?" asked Jolson as he left his chair.

Purviance walked stiffly to a doorway. "The actual membership figures of Group A, Mr. Janeway, are security restricted. I can tell you this. We have lots of members."

"Many of them on the island here with you?"

"Yes sir, quite a few," said Purviance. "All heavily armed and very loyal. I'd say my isle is . . ."

"Impregnable?"

"Yes sir, just about."

TWENTY-FIVE

THE storage room was chill and pastoral. Mist trailed from Purviance's slot mouth as he said, "The wall paintings were my father's idea. Except for the designs, the storage rooms are all pretty much the same." The stalk of dry grass fell from his lip and rested on his trouser bib. "This particular one is sylvan. We also have desert, jungle, famous moments in Earth history, etcetera. And one cute room with fuzzy animals painted on the walls."

Jolson studied the cold low room. "Why?"

"Well sir, it cheered my father up I guess. He never exactly told me his reasons." Purviance touched a cubicle door. There were two dozen doors, in rows on the walls. "If you had all the rooms simply white you might get the notion you were shrunk and spending your days inside a refrigerator. Father preferred looking at sheep and fellows with crooked sticks, I figure."

Jolson turned his head. "Where are your Group A guards, Purviance, the ones with the guns?"

"You can't see them, no sir," said Purviance. "They see you, you can bet. I have them cleverly concealed behind the paneling." He tapped his fingers one at a time in sequence on the cubicle door. "In this particular bin we have, let me see, a famous boccie ball player. Waiting."

Grimacing against the cold, Jolson edged slowly closer to the Group A leader. "For how long?"

"The orders are to defrost him at the beginning of the next century, at the start of the boccie ball season," said Purviance. "Our thawing rooms are on the next level down. Those we'll see in a minute, Mr. Janeway. Notice how I'm still maintaining the illusion of polite equality. Mr. Janeway."

"Yes sir," said Jolson. He moved, slid between Purviance and a solid slice of wall. He bent an arm around the man's throat and spun him so the front of Purviance was shielding him and his back was flat against the pastoral murals.

"Hey now, Mr. Janeway." His pipe snapped from his mouth and hit the frigid floor.

"Okay, first I want Jennifer Hark. Then the War Bureau members you've kidnaped, Purviance. If you've got a Sensible Friendly Publishing Company fanzine reporter stored here, I want him also. Order them all thawed out and brought here."

"Stop throttling me or I'll order you rayed to death."

"That would get you as well," said Jolson, increasing the pressure on Purviance's throat and fighting down the Group A leader's clutching hands.

"There is that."

Jolson said, "Let's go. Tell your men to gather in here. All of them, or as many as can fit. I want all their weapons turned in. Otherwise I'll finish you and stick you in one of your own bins."

"Don't talk about creepy things like that," said Purviance. "I told you I get the willies. You say you want all my men to surrender?"

"We can start with the ones behind the walls here. How many are there?"

Purviance tried to cough. "You're that Chameleon Corps fellow, am I right?"

Jolson tightened his hold. "Now."

"Well sir, I'd better explain something to you."

"Give the orders, then explain."

"There's a monitoring mike in each storage room, which picks up my voice." Purviance called out, "Come into the sylvan room, Rackstraw. You, too, Tyler. Get Hockering."

The entrance door swung open and the tattooed man in the shaggy overcoat entered, a blaster rifle held in front of him. "Trouble?"

"Drop the rifle," said Jolson.

"Let loose a little," said Purviance. "Yes sir, Rackstraw, drop the rifle."

A thin blond man followed Rackstraw into the cold room and tossed a real straw broom next to the rifle the bearded guard had let go of. "I don't go around armed. My job is mostly cleaning up." He took a position against a wall, shuffling and rubbing his elbows.

"Where's the rest of your group?"

"Well sir, that's what I'm trying to explain. We're on a sort of a skeleton crew basis here. Rackstraw, Tyler, Hockering now, myself and Mrs. Nash, who fixes our meals and does the mending."

"Don't try to con me, Purviance. Group A isn't made up of four guys and a cook."

Purviance said, "We have lots more members. It's only that few of them live in. See, most of the money, let's be frank about it, we make off the freezing and storage business goes right out to pay for kidnapers and assassins. We have to bribe politicians, too, and all kinds of officials. Everyone doesn't share my burning passion for Earth supremacy. So I have to pay, through the nose, for loyalty. What with one thing and another, well sir, I really don't have the budget to maintain a large standing army or a big resident staff. The food bill alone would break me at this point. Taking over the universe, even this little one, that can cost."

"You really don't have an army?"

"That will come. I know once I've assimilated all the major war minds in the Barnum System, and then in all systems, once I have swallowed up all the best war planning geniuses, then I won't have any trouble. I'll have such a war machine, such a propaganda wing that thousands will flock to the just cause of Earth supremacy. Yes sir."

"Right now, though, it's you guys and Mrs. Nash?"

"Well, yes."

"Then you're not even much of a threat, only a nuisance," said Jolson. "You're not even a pacifist. You're just another nitwit."

Purviance suddenly backed into Jolson and took his wind. Purviance flew hands first toward the floor and scooped up the surrendered rifle. He braced it against a knee, pointed dead up at Jolson. "Nitwit perhaps. Still this gun will fix you, you off-planet scum. I won't even bother putting you in storage. You I'll kill out and out and fling in my lake."

"Don't," said Rackstraw. From his overcoat sleeve he'd fished a blaster pistol. He triggered it and the rifle was sizzled out of Purviance's hands. "Up against the bins, Purviance. No more fooling around."

"Hey now, Rackstraw," said Purviance, puzzled, stroking his wrists both at once.

To Jolson the shaggy tattooed man said, "15–6–1–24–26–9–6."

"You Political Espionage guys," said Jolson. "When did you get in here?"

"I replaced the genuine Rackstraw during the night, two nights ago. The Political Espionage Office may not be the Chameleon Corps, but when it comes to faking a beard and tattooing myself by moonlight, I don't need a course at any Academy."

"So why didn't you clear all this up and save me the trouble?"

"Don't get angry, Jolson. I was sent in on orders from Head Mickens on Barnum, once we figured out where the seat of Group A was likely to be. My instructions were to give you ample time to infiltrate and make your play, and to back you up."

"How about Jennifer?"

"They have her in a storage room two doors over from this one," said the PEO agent. "I didn't want to risk thawing her until you arrived and we had the whole thing sewn up."

"Damn," said Nat Hockering at the open doorway. "Outnumbered by the lousy authorities." He grunted and ran off.

"We'll get him later," said Jolson. "Is that really all the rest of the staff?"

"Yes," said the fake Rackstraw. "Except for the cook, and I bribed her over on our side yesterday after lunch."

"That explains the poison," muttered Purviance.

"Her own idea," said the PEO man.

"Take us to Jennifer Hark, Purviance," said Jolson. "I want her brought back now."

"Shouldn't we think about Dean Swift first?" put in the Political Espionage man. "He is the top man in the War Bureau after all."

Jolson got Purviance by the arm. "Jennifer first."

The drawer lid had sun-bright Joshua trees decorating it. "In there she is," said Purviance, his stubby hand on the handle. "Sealed in a plyo shroud. We can whip her out, put her on a hand truck, and whisk her down to reclaim. She'll be up and around in a matter of minutes. That's part of the exclusive patented Purviance method. Quick thaw, quick reclaim, no nasty side effects."

"Okay, okay," said Jolson. He put his hand over Purviance's and together they slid the drawer out.

"Well sir," said Purviance. "That's a funny one."

The drawer was empty.

TWENTY-SIX

T H E Political Espionage agent came over and stared into the empty bin. "That's the right drawer, Jolson."

Jolson said, "Hockering maybe."

"Sure," said the fake Rackstraw. "There's a strong possibility he grabbed her to use as a hostage."

"Where would he take her? Where's reclaim?"

"Downstairs," said Purviance. "You'll notice an arrow pointing off the hall here."

Jolson said, "Okay, Rackstraw, you get the War Bureau dusted off, and anyone else he's snatched. I'll find Jennifer."

"Take this," said the PEO agent. He slid another pistol out of another overcoat sleeve and pressed it into Jolson's palm.

There was no one in the warm brown reclaim room. All of its three doors were closed. Jolson made a running search. He stopped by a cocoa-colored medical table and frowned, bent closer to the table. "Golliwog," he said.

At the exit door marked TUNNEL he picked up a strong touch of the scent again, Jennifer's perfume. He opened the door carefully, pistol ready. There didn't seem to be anything beyond it except long, long darkness. Jolson watched the dark until it gradually formed into damp metal walls. Footsteps echoed far down the tunnel. Jolson entered.

Beneath each ear a pressure was growing. Jolson took a deep swallowing breath, paused to listen again. No one was moving in the tunnel now. He hesitated, then continued. He felt he was beyond the isle now, under the lake.

Five minutes further into the darkness and he sensed the perfume again. Close by. He threw himself down to the tunnel floor and at the same moment a blaster crackled, slicing harshly through the air where he had been.

A hand lantern flashed on and caught him in its cast. "Who the hell are you?" asked Hockering's voice.

Jolson kept his eyes focused below the glare of the lantern. The pistol was still in his right hand. He came to his knees, waiting for a chance to use it. "I just joined Group A. Looks like PEO is taking over upstairs and I'm escaping."

The big man took shape behind the lantern. And next to him Jennifer, alive. "Wait, I know that face," said Hockering.

In the glow of the lantern Jolson was shorter than Janeway, younger. His face was lean, weathered slightly. His hair was close-cropped and his nose faintly hooked. "You probably do," he said.

"Sure, I saw pictures we got from our guy on Barnum. You're Jolson, with your real face on."

"That's right, Hockering."

"Good enough. I can do you in, Jolson, and really see who I'm killing." A pistol showed next to the lantern.

"No," said Jennifer. She slapped both her hands out of the darkness and Hockering's pistol clanked to the tunnel floor.

"You dumb skinny bitch," said Hockering. "Don't go

smacking my pistol away when I'm trying to kill somebody."
He reared the lantern up to strike her.

Jolson watched the lantern rise to the height of its arc.
He watched its light illuminate Hockering's head and
chest. Jolson exhaled, took aim. He shot the lantern from
the man's grasp, stepped quickly ahead and knocked Hockering over with his free hand. Another blow and the
Nepenthe attendant was unconscious. "Hi, Jennifer. You
okay?"

"Yes, considering." The girl laughed, sniffed. Came and
hugged Jolson. "Thanks, Ben. Yes, I'm okay." She moved
away, retrieved the lantern and got it working again. "I
thought for a second there you might kill Hockering."

"There was no need," said Jolson. He ripped off Hockering's shirt, tore it into strips and tied the man up se-
curely.

"What about Purviance, Ben?"

"One of your PEO daredevils got into the island, too.
He's running the thawing operation and herding Purviance." Jolson sat Hockering up against the tunnel's cool
damp wall, turned to Jennifer. "Are you sure you're not
hurt?"

"No, really."

"You do get drugged and frozen more than most girls,"
said Jolson. "Why I worry. Where does this tunnel lead?"

"Other side of the lake. There's nothing but forest and
wilds there. Hockering was going to hide out, keep me
around as a hostage for a while, in case he was trailed."

"Your Political Espionage man can handle things up in
the Purviance works for a while. There turns out not to be
a very large Group A in residence. Let's go take a look at
the forest. You need some fresh air and sunshine."

"Right," said the girl, her grin sharp in the lantern light. "We don't necessarily have to talk shop now, but what was Purviance and his Group A up to exactly, Ben?"

As they walked together toward the tunnel's end Jolson told her and finally said, "That damned Purviance. I was hoping he really might have a way to stop some of the wars."

"That won't happen, probably ever."

The tunnel stopped and outside its metal gates was a thick endless forest, still bright in the afternoon. Jolson opened the gates. "He was just another nitwit."

"Why," asked Jennifer, stepping onto soft grass, "did you decide to change when you came after us?"

Jolson said, "I don't know, Jennifer. It just happened."

"You really are," said the girl, catching his hand, "Ben Jolson now, then?"

"What?"

"The way you look. You're yourself?" she asked.

Jolson reached up and touched his face. "As a matter of fact," he said, "yes."